FREAKY FLYDAY

OTHER RAVENSPELL BOOKS
BY DAVID FARLAND:

Of Mice and Magic

The Wizard of Ooze

FREAKY FLYDAY

BOOK THREE RAVENSPELL BOOK THREE

DAVID FARLAND

Covenant Communications, Inc.

Illustration © Howard Lyon

Published by Covenant Communications, Inc.
American Fork, Utah

Copyright © 2009 by David Farland

Printed in Canada
First Printing: September 2009

16 15 14 13 12 11 10 09   10 9 8 7 6 5 4 3 2 1

ISBN-13 978-1-59811-667-0
ISBN-10 1-59811-667-3

For Braiden Norton, Serena Doering, and all of my special fans everywhere!

TABLE OF CONTENTS

CHAPTER I

THE BLACK LOTUS

Never celebrate the demise of evil;
for it is when we least expect it that it is
most likely to surface in a new form.
—RUFUS FLYCATCHER

"Look, we're on television!" Ben shouted.

Ben's mom had just turned on the tube while Ben and two dozen of his mouse friends waited for their pizza to cool. There was Ben on the screen, larger than life, clutching his little spear made from a needle, his helm carved from a walnut shell looking like some spooky skull, his whiskers twitching.

A newsman said, "And here is the ultimatum given from a mouse who claims he was once human . . ."

Ben spoke into the camera. "I'm going to teach mice how to use spears and stuff, so that they can protect themselves. There are a lot of mice in pet shops all over the world. They're being fed to snakes and lizards and stuff, and so me and the other mice are going to come and set them free. If you don't like that—tough.

"You know, you could just save us all some trouble. Free the mice in your pet shops. Free the mice, now!"

For a moment, the picture froze on Ben, and a sign came up beneath him saying BENJAMIN RAVENSPELL.

"Gol," Ben said. "I'm famous!" He'd been hoping that when his mom turned on the TV, she'd flip on some cartoons, but seeing himself was even better.

"Oh, Ben," Amber shouted with glee, "you look sooo handsome!"

Ben beamed and peered around the house. It felt so strange to be home again after nearly two weeks in the wild.

Yet in those two weeks, everything in the world had changed. Ben had turned into a mouse, and he'd had adventures that would have made him faint from terror not long ago. He'd faced lizards as big as dinosaurs and kittens that seemed larger than lions. He'd taken a ride through a hailstorm on the back of an insane bat, and had fought off giant Wyoming thunder worms.

Ben had grown inside, yet it wasn't just him who had changed. He peered around, wondering at the difference, and suddenly saw it all at once. The whole house was clean—spotless!

His mother had washed the dishes and

mopped the floor. She'd gotten a perm and had brushed her teeth.

It appeared as if his mom only cleaned the house when she was stressed out. With Ben gone, she'd been filled with nervous energy, and now the house was immaculate!

Gone was the old Christmas tree in the corner; gone were the dust bunnies; gone were the ants and the cockroaches.

Only one little ant could be seen, a miserable fellow lumbering over the carpet. As he hunted vainly for food, he sang,

> Life ain't no fun,
> When you can't find a crumb!
> I'm just one little guy,
> With ten thousand eyes.
> And them eyes can't see
> Any food for me.
> So I'll keep wan-der-un,
> Searchin' for a crumb.

In some ways, it didn't even feel like home anymore, and Ben didn't feel like Ben. Yet he was relieved to be safe, out of the harsh weather, with a pizza the size of a football field cooling on the table.

His mom had suddenly become more accepting of mice.

Last time she'd seen mice in the house, she'd sucked them up with a vacuum cleaner. Now she was catering to their every whim, even if she did look a little freaked out about it.

She was sitting on a sofa, watching the mice on her couch with an odd smile, sort of twitching from nervousness. Every muscle was rigid.

Meanwhile, Ben's dad, Butch, had flopped into his own chair to watch television, lost to the world, as if he were watching a football game. Nothing could faze him.

The television announcer, a dark-haired woman with a sly smile, said, "We now continue with our coverage of the mouse that shook the world today." The mice on the couch all cheered. Lady Blackpool, a sorceress shrew, had cast a spell on all of the mice so that they could understand human speech. "World reaction to the news has been swift and in some cases harsh . . ."

Suddenly the television showed a bearded man with a black robe and a black turban wrapped around his head. "We in Iran are not women to be frightened by mice," he thundered in a thick Arab accent. "We do not take orders from American vermin. We are ready to fight with Weapons of Mouse Destruction! Down with the infidel America! Down with mice!" He raised a machine gun into the air with one hand and fired off a salvo of bullets.

The camera switched pictures again, showing a beautiful woman in an evening gown. "Meanwhile, in France, the prime minister has already named an ambassador to the mice of the world and is suing for peace."

The beautiful woman held a bottle of champagne in one hand and white cheese in the other.

"We are eager to establish diplomatic relation-ships with the nation of Mouse-adonia," she said in a kind, educated voice with a hint of an accent that sounded more English than French. "We will gladly offer reparations for past wrongs. In World War II, mice gnawed through the wires of German tanks hiding in our cornfields, disabling them, and so lent us aid in our struggle. We owe our freedom to mice. Perhaps the whole world owes its freedom to mice! Certainly we must return the favor. We here in France look forward to developing strong diplomatic ties to mouse-kind."

The anchorwoman reappeared on screen. "Meanwhile, the reaction at home is mixed." A sen-ator from Arkansas was shown mugging for the cam-era. "Free the mice? They want civil rights for mice? What if we give them equal rights? Where does it stop? Human rights should just be for humans. Next thing you know, chickens will want to vote, and hamsters will be demanding health care!"

The television switched pictures once more.

Harold Shortzenbeggar, the tan and muscular governor of California, was suddenly shown with a crowd of people at his back. "We, the people of California, proudly offer our hand in fellowship to the mice of our state, and hereby immediately grant them all of the rights given to any citizen.

"From this day forward, it will be illegal to hold a mouse captive, to injure a mouse, or to commit any foul deed against a mouse. All mice are to be freed from pet shops, private homes, and research facilities at once.

"Mice are our friends. Mice are our brothers. I like mice!" He held up a small white mouse for the cameras.

The poor mouse of course had no idea what was going on. It squeaked in terror, shouting, "Help! Help! He's pulling my tail!" but of course the governor didn't understand mouse.

Governor Shortzenbeggar turned and set the mouse down in the grass. The camera pulled back to reveal a character in a Mickey Mouse suit behind the governor, waving to the world.

"Now," Governor Shortzenbeggar said, "let's all go to Disneyland!" The crowd clapped and cheered.

Meanwhile, a bunch of news anchormen shouted at the governor, "Does this mean that mice will be granted access to public education?" "Will they be eligible to get driver's licenses?" The governor ignored the questions.

"And there you have it," the anchorwoman said. "The governor of California *officially* freeing the mice!"

"Hooray!" Ben shouted. Other mice raised their voices and cheered too, but Amber just peered about, her eyes filling with tears of gratitude.

Not all of the creatures on the couch were mice. Bushmaster the vole and many of his friends from the wild were there, too. Voles look like mice, but unlike mice, which eat just about anything, voles only eat vegetables and seeds. And though they were not mice, and had never been caged like mice, the truth was that they looked so much like mice that they often suffered the same fate—being poisoned by humans or caught in traps.

The voles cheered and leapt about. Only one other figure among them was silent, the gray-furred shrew, Lady Blackpool, who bent her head in thought.

"You have done well, Amber," Lady Blackpool said softly, "and you are to be congratulated. The fame of your deeds has spread far and wide, and you have gone a long way toward reaching your destiny. The humans of the world have already begun freeing the mice that have so long been held captive.

"I imagine that all across the world, human children are freeing the mice that have been kept as pets for generations.

"Yet I worry at what you have done."

Amber's ears drew back in alarm, and she stood up, whiskers twitching as if she were trying to catch the scent of some enemy. "What do you mean? What are you worried about?"

"You have freed many mice," Lady Blackpool confirmed. "The humans will let them out of their cages. But have you considered what will happen now? Your cousins will be loosed into a world fraught with dangers—cats and snakes, traps and owls. They won't know where to live, how to protect themselves, or how to feed themselves. I worry for them—the white mice most of all. With their fur color, they won't be able to hide from predators."

"Oh, no!" Amber said. "I hadn't thought of that."

Ben's elation suddenly faded. He really liked Amber, and he was proud of what they had done in behalf of mice around the world. But now Lady Blackpool had ruined his taste of victory. He felt bad for Amber most of all. She had a good heart, and it wasn't right to blame her for the fate of all the mice in the world.

An old pet shop mouse named Barley Beard spoke up. "'It's better to die free than to live in captivity!' At least, that's what I always say!"

Lady Blackpool was much smaller than Barley Beard, but she stared at him so pointedly that she seemed to grow. "That is a choice that *you* might make for yourself, but you should not make it for others."

"Oh, what shall I do?" Amber cried, bewildered.

"There is nothing that you can do now," Lady Blackpool said. "You've squandered your mage dust, and you will be powerless until you've gathered more. That was not done wisely, my friend. The first rule of magic is, 'Always keep some power in reserve.'"

Ben peered at Amber, who began to tremble as if she would cry. Wizards drew their magical energy from something called "mage dust." The stuff was invisible, but apparently it was everywhere. As a familiar, Ben attracted mage dust just like a magnet draws iron shavings. Then Amber drew the power from him to cast her spells.

But with all of their mage dust used up in their last battle, Amber was powerless. She was like a battery that had lost its charge. She couldn't do anything to help the mice of the world at that moment.

Amber's eyes moistened. She was almost in tears. "But . . . Ben asked me to cast that spell, turning that madman into a worm and then a dung beetle."

"General Crawley was evil," Ben shouted. "He was going to blow us all up!"

Lady Blackpool said softly, "There were other ways to stop him—ways that would have used far less mage dust. Amber, just because a friend asks you to do something does not mean that you should do it. If Ben asked you to stick your tongue on a frozen fire hydrant, would you do so?"

Amber was a naïve mouse. She had no idea what would happen if she stuck her tongue to a frozen fire hydrant, so she answered bravely, "Yes, if Ben asked me to!"

Lady Blackpool chuckled. "I suppose that you would, and all too soon you would regret it. Amber, you're a kind mouse, but there is a saying at our wizard's school: 'Kindness that is not tempered by wisdom is often kindness wasted.'"

"But, what about the mice that I've set free?" Amber asked. "How will I save them?"

Lady Blackpool answered thoughtfully, "Great things have been set in motion, my dear, and the wheels of time roll on. The mice of the world are scattered so far and wide that neither you nor anyone else can protect them. I suppose that there is not much that we can do now. Sometimes we cannot depend on others. Sometimes we must save ourselves or die in the attempt.

"You have given the mice of the world a great opportunity. Let us hope that they use it wisely, that they band together for their own safety, and that they survive."

"You can't let yourself feel guilty," Ben told Amber. "Lady Blackpool is right. Some mice are going to be set free, and they might have some bad luck afterward. But it's better than being fed to some kid's snakes or lizards. In time, your name will be remembered by all mice everywhere. You'll be famous forever!"

"You know," a young vole named Meadowsweet offered. "I think that pizza has cooled down enough to eat."

Another vole, one of Ben's friends named Bushmaster, reached out with one paw and touched it. "Yessss!" he said, and then he dived onto the pizza.

The small creatures all shouted, "Hooray," and followed Bushmaster, some voles racing to eat mushrooms and olives while the mice grabbed paws full of cheese and pepperoni.

As the small folk all went into a feeding frenzy, the television continued to play. News anchors wondered aloud what kinds of powers Amber might harbor. "She turned a nuclear bomb into fireworks," one said. "What kind of threat does such a creature pose to the world?"

"I agree," another commentator said. "Two hours ago, the United States was the ultimate power on this planet. Now, it appears that a mouse may soon be dictating terms of surrender to our president."

Ben wondered at that. Amber didn't seem to be interested in trying to be queen of the world. But the newsmen did have a point. She was more powerful than he'd ever imagined. Even Amber didn't seem to have a clue what she might be able to do.

Yet she didn't have the energy right now to turn him back into a human. For the next three days, Ben was still vulnerable.

Ben wandered away from the television, away from the other mice. He heard a congressman saying that perhaps Amber should be arrested on charges of witchcraft, but Ben knew that that was silly. She had power, but it wasn't evil.

People don't know it, Ben thought, *but if they wanted to, they could kill Amber right now.*

He clawed his way up the back of the couch, his paws sinking into tiny snags in the fabric, and then leapt up onto the windowsill and stood looking out.

Silent clouds slid like ghosts beneath a silver moon. All of the houses on his street were dark and empty, with a haunted look.

A militia had planned on nuking this neighborhood earlier in the day, until Amber saved it. So everyone had left their homes.

Now it seemed that the people were returning: out on the road, headlights from cars were slashing at the darkness, the lights spilling out onto the roads like milk. A truck pulled up across the street. It was a news truck with a satellite dish on top. Some men got out and a reporter began speaking into a microphone as she pointed at Ben's house.

The telephone rang, and Ben's dad, Butch, picked it up. He listened to someone on the other end for a moment. "An interview on *Good Morning America?* How much do you pay?" He hesitated then said, "Call back with a better offer!" He slammed the phone down.

We're going to be famous, Ben thought. He looked down the road at the long line of head-lights in the distance. More reporters were coming. Lots more.

Ben rubbed his paws through his long whiskers and blinked, trembling with nervous energy.

It won't be long until I'm human again, he reassured himself. *Amber will turn me back into a human soon.*

But he couldn't bring himself to hope anymore. He was a mouse, and right now it felt as if he might be stuck being a mouse forever, even though he had good reason to hope.

"Mom," Ben said, "we need to get out of the house for a couple of days. Amber can't cast any more spells until we gather some mage dust, and we can't do that if we're just sitting here."

Ben's mom peered at him with a frightened look. She obviously didn't relish the idea of taking a bunch of mice out on a road trip.

"Where would we go?" Butch asked.

"I don't know," Ben said. "Anywhere, I guess."

"How about Disneyland?" Ben's mom suggested.

Ben's heart pounded for joy. He'd always wanted to go there, but his mom had always said that they were too poor.

"That would cost a lot of money," Butch said. "Our credit cards are all maxed out."

Suddenly a tiny spider came crawling up the back of the couch.

"Hiya, Ben," the spider said.

"Cob!" Ben whispered in surprise. "How are you doing?" Cob was a little spider that lived in Ben's garage. Ben had met the strange fellow when Ben had first been turned into a mouse. Cob had warned Ben that an evil bat was going to try to stop him from reaching the pet shop to free the mice there. Cob had told how all of the spiders in the area were betting that Ben would never make it to the pet shop alive.

Ben had seen the flies that Cob won in the bet. There were about a million of them stacked on the floor in Ben's garage. Ben's mom was really freaked out about it. Ben's dad had already asked why his garage was filled five feet deep with dead flies, but Ben had pretended that he didn't know. He didn't want to get Cob in trouble.

"I've got a message for your friend there," Cob said, nodding toward Amber. "It just came in on the web."

The "web" was the worldwide web, a vast spider web with strands that reached everywhere. The spiders could talk on it by plunking a strand, sending vibrations all around the world.

"A message from who?" Ben asked.

"A bullfrog named Rufus Flycatcher," Cob answered. Ben knew the name. Rufus Flycatcher was a wizard famous in the animal world. He ran a magic school called S.W.A.R.M.—the Small Wizard's Academy of Restorative Magic—out in some swamps, far, far away. "This Flycatcher fellow says, 'You must warn Amber immediately. Danger is brewing. Prepare for war. The black lotus has bloomed!'"

Black lotus? Ben wondered. He had no idea what the message meant.

He only hoped that Lady Blackpool might understand the significance of it.

CHAPTER 2

SHADOW OF THE
EVER SHADE

*The shape of the future is defined by
what we do today. Our limits today are
bound by what we have accomplished in the past.
For this reason, each day we should struggle to
make a better tomorrow.*
—LADY BLACKPOOL

Lady Blackpool climbed up on the armrest of the couch, while down below her on the cushions the mice and voles stood in a crowd, waiting for her to reveal the meaning behind Rufus Flycatcher's vague message.

The festive mood of the evening was quite ruined. There had been talk of war, and Amber felt weary to the core of her soul. The pizza on the couch lay cooling, its cheese drying as hard as cement, while outside the window strange lights flashed as news camera crews continued to gather. Every ten seconds the telephone would ring, and Ben's father was making a game of looking at the

15

caller ID, demanding more money for an interview, then hanging up.

The phone rang, and Ben's dad said, "Say, Ben, some publisher wants to know if you'll write a book about your adventures as a mouse!"

"Oh, wow, I don't know, Dad," Ben said. "My cursive isn't very good."

"He says he'll pay you three million dollars," Butch said, a smile creeping across his face.

Ben's eyes widened in surprise.

"Is that a lot?" Amber asked.

"We'd have more than enough to go to Disneyland!" Ben said.

"We'll take the deal," Butch cried with glee. "I'll want half of that in our bank account in the morning."

The person on the other end of the line began talking excitedly.

"Movie rights?" Butch said. "No, those don't come with it!"

The person on the other end began to shout frantically.

"Call back when you've got a serious offer!" Butch demanded; he slammed the phone down and pulled the plug, turning to listen to what Lady Blackpool had to say.

Ben sat staring at his dad in shock. Amber could tell that Ben felt terrible about losing millions of dollars.

Lady Blackpool stood up on the arm of the sofa on her back legs, her front paws folded over her white tummy. Benjamin Ravenspell's parents leaned near her. Earlier in the evening, Amber had cast a spell that let humans understand both her and Ben when they spoke, and so the humans knew that something was up.

Now Lady Backpool addressed the group, and she must have cast her own spell, because Benjamin Ravenspell's parents grew very attentive.

"Once every so often," Lady Blackpool began, "great evil arises—the kind of evil that is so monstrous, so powerful, and so malignant that all of the good folks in the world must stand together in order to resist it."

"How often does this happen?" Amber asked. "Once a week?" Lady Blackpool's tone had confused her. After all, Amber had been forced to save the world twice in the short time since she had broken free from her cage.

"Not once a week, or even once every hundred years," Lady Blackpool said. "I am speaking of a great evil, an earth-shattering evil—the kind of evil that might come only once every thousand years if we are lucky."

"Ooooh," Meadowsweet whispered in awe.

"In ages past," Lady Blackpool continued, "the good folk were taken by surprise. A consortium of evil sorcerers seized control and ruled the world for ten thousand years!"

"Humph!" Benjamin Ravenspell's dad said. "I never heard of anything like that. It's not in any history books that I know of." Ben's dad was a small man, very muscular. His head was bald, but he had a huge handlebar mustache. He had tattoos on his neck.

"It happened long ago," Lady Blackpool explained, "before there were such things as history books. These sorcerers were animals mostly, led by an evil human, the Ever Shade, he was called.

"He was human in form, but his soul was void of the wisdom and kindness that humans should possess. He ruled in a land across the sea, and he kept the whole world in ignorance. Those who could not read or write could not pass on the lore of the Ever Shade, so none of your human books tell of him.

"But surely he haunts the dreams of mankind still. Look into your mind, into your nightmares, and you will see his face—a man dressed in black robes, with a hood pulled deep. No flesh covers the bone-white horror of his visage, so that when you see him, you will see only a grinning skull. That is the Ever Shade."

Amber felt a chill rise up her spine. She had seen dead zombie mice in the lair of the evil worm Sebaceous Ooze. The mice had slaved for him even though they lived no more. This Ever Shade sounded like a zombie, too.

"Are you saying that the Ever Shade will be coming back?" Ben's mother asked.

"Yes," Lady Blackpool replied, "we must watch for him. Though his body died long ago, his magic was as deep as his malice, and many times he has sought to return. What form he will take—animal or human—I cannot know. Nor do we know exactly *when* he will come.

"But long ago, the good wizards of the world

planted a flower deep in the swamps, a flower that is guarded to this very day by fearsome alligators. It is the black lotus, and it blooms only when our nemesis is about to take bodily form."

"So this black lotus," Butch asked, "is like some kind of meter, one that tells us how much evil is in the world?"

"You could put it that way," Lady Blackpool said.

"So the Ever Shade is here?" Ben said. "He's alive already?"

"Not yet, but soon," Lady Blackpool said. "Somewhere soon he will be born."

"Where?" Amber asked, casting her eyes about fearfully.

"He could arise anywhere—" Lady Blackpool said, "on a far continent or across the street or upstairs beneath your bed . . ."

The threat sent a chill through Amber as she imagined what might be hiding beneath Ben's bed.

Lady Blackpool hesitated for a moment and then added, "If history is any indicator, our enemy does not yet pose a great threat. He will bide his time and gather his supporters—lesser sorcerers that grant him aid."

"After he's born, he'll need time to grow," Ben said hopefully. "It could be *years* before he's grown."

"Humans take years to grow," Lady Blackpool objected, "but most animals reach maturity in only a few weeks. Some mature in a matter of hours. What form the Ever Shade will choose this time, we cannot know."

"I'll be ready for him," Amber said.

"You're not even close to being ready," Lady Blackpool said. "Together you and Ben have great power, but you don't know how to use it. You must go to S.W.A.R.M., the Small Wizard's Academy of Restorative Magic. We can only hope that there you can gain the wisdom and skills that you need to defeat the Ever Shade."

"But . . . I'm not going to S.W.A.R.M," Ben objected. "Amber promised to turn me back into a human. I have my own school. I have things that I want to do with my life!"

Amber grew nervous at that. She liked Ben a lot. He was strong and brave and handsome. She *had* promised to turn him back into a human, though.

But suddenly she wondered if that was a good idea.

Maybe I should keep him, Amber thought, *as a pet*.

It only seemed like the natural thing to do. Humans had been keeping mice as pets for thousands of years.

Why shouldn't I be able to keep him? Amber wondered.

"What would you do with your life, Benjamin Ravenspell?" Lady Blackpool asked. "What *great* thing would you accomplish? The world needs you to go to S.W.A.R.M. Would you rather spend your days watching television and playing video games?

"How sad! People talk as if their lives have

great value, but then they waste them minute by minute, spending their hours and days in frivolous pursuits."

Amber peered hard at Ben. He was a handsome mouse, the handsomest mouse she had ever seen. He was brave and bold and wise in ways that other mice were not, and he had a goodness to him that ran to the core of his soul.

But he wasn't a mouse—not really. He had been born as a human, and it seemed right that he be one.

He wasn't a mouse by nature.

But that could change, Amber told herself.

CHAPTER 3

THE FRUITCAKE AND THE FLY

*No one really knows what is possible and what is not,
for the universe is far stranger than we dream.*
—THORN THE MOUSE

Two thousand years ago the Greek philosopher Aristotle observed that life can come from practically nowhere. To prove his point, he placed a bit of fig in an earthenware urn for three days and then opened the lid. To the astonishment of his students, a single fruit fly was perched upon the rotting fig.

Thus Aristotle formed the theory of "spontaneous generation," the idea that life could arise from inanimate objects.

Unfortunately, it was an idea that lost popularity. Further experiments showed that every animal and plant had to have a father and mother of some sort, and it was assumed that Aristotle's fly must have come from an egg that had been laid by a mother fly before he placed the fig in the urn.

But of course, the know-it-all scientists were wrong, and on the night that Ben Ravenspell sat in his home listening to dire tales of the Ever Shade, Aristotle's fly was reborn.

It happened this way: 666 years earlier, in a small coastal fishing village in England called Hartlepoole, a young woman was baking a fruit-cake for her mother-in-law. The young woman detested her mother-in-law but felt obligated to give her something. It was the day before Christmas, and of course the young wife had to give her mother-in-law *something,* and so by age-old tradition she prepared to give her that most hated of holiday fare—a fruitcake.

Now, it is a well-known fact that no one likes fruitcake. Fruitcakes are nasty in taste, completely indigestible, lacking in sustenance, and most of them are as hard as a brick. The only people who ever get fooled into eating them are very young children who take one bite and then spit the rest of the fruitcake into their napkins if they are polite—or just discharge it onto the floor if they are not.

Yet each year for a thousand years, people have given fruitcakes away at Christmas. Only heaven knows why anyone would give such a thing. Some of the loathsome cakes are obviously foisted off as this one was meant to be—as *pretend* gifts.

The young wife was too frightened of her mother-in-law to tell the old nag that she wished her dead, and so she made an abominable cake instead.

But fruitcakes are seldom eaten. Most of these indigestible lumps of moldering mash are simply regifted. A person gets one, doesn't know what to do with it, thinks it's too valuable to throw away or fools herself into thinking that "someone must like them," and so hands it off to an unfortunate soul that she neither cares about nor respects, usually with a little handwritten message that says, "I baked this cake using my grandmother's favorite recipe. Merry Christmas!"

And in fact, that miserable young wife in Hartlepoole wrote just such a note: "I made this for ye in mine grand dame's favourite manner. May ye be of goode cheere upon this, the Holiest of Days!"

So she wrote the note, set the fruitcake into a cloth bag to cool, and then went out on her back porch to watch the sunset. She had only just taken her seat when her neighbor's black cat came loping across the lawn with a nice fat mouse in its jaws. The mouse was obviously still alive, for its little feet were kicking, and it squeaked in terror. The woman knew that the cat liked to torment mice before it killed them, and so she decided to take action.

"Naughty cat!" the woman scolded, reaching over and grabbing the cat's tail. "Spew ye that mouse out! Spew it, or the devil'll have ye!"

Just then, an elderly monk happened to be walking down the lane, herding a little lost lamb with his shepherd's crook. He spotted the woman talking to the cat, heard her mention the devil, and immediately raised a mob and had the poor young wife put on trial for witchcraft—for in those days, it was believed that only a witch would talk to a black cat.

In the course of the trial, the woman was tied to a stone and was to be thrown into the ocean. If she sank, it was a sign that she was innocent and could be properly mourned. If she floated, it was a sign that she was a witch and would then be suitably hanged.

So the city's executioner (really just the butcher doing double duty, looking very grim and medieval in his black hood), tied a millstone about her neck and prepared to shove her off the city docks, into the ocean.

"Ye are all idiots," the housewife shouted, "and someday the world will know it!"

The townsfolk all "oohed" and "aahed" at the pronouncement, for it sounded like a witch's curse. Then the housewife fainted, and the executioner shoved her and the millstone into the water.

She sank, of course, and the townsfolk were left to mourn.

But little did they realize that this woman did indeed have magical powers, and it was in that very same village that the curse took effect. It was many years later when it happened. In 1798, the French madman Napoleon was on the march, trying to take over the world, when a huge storm arose and crashed one of his warships onto the rocks near Hartlepoole.

The sole survivor of that horrible wreck was an ape that had been captured in Africa and had been taken as a pet by the captain. The ape swam to shore, and the townsfolk caught it.

No one in the village had ever seen a Frenchman, so they mistook the poor ape as a French spy, and the townsfolk put it on trial. The ape refused to answer any questions. When put on the witness stand, it would do nothing but make rude noises. Then it snatched away the judge's white powdered wig and raced around the courtroom, terrifying the public.

So the ape was hanged, and the village of Hartlepoole gained such a reputation for its stupidity that for the next two hundred years it became home to the world-renowned International Village Idiots' Convention, a place where morons and imbeciles of all ilk could meet, frolic, exchange dumb ideas, and perhaps find some like-minded halfwit to marry.

But as for the fruitcake—well, when the young wife was hanged, her grieving husband came home that night and found it with the note, so he gave it to his mother.

She wisely refused to eat it, and regifted it—along with the handwritten note—to a friend, who placed it in her cupboard as a deterrent to rats.

The following Christmas, the friend bestowed it upon a neighbor, who sent it to the far side of England to a sister who didn't want it either.

In fact, it was just that fruitcake's good fortune that for 666 years it got palmed off from one unloved neighbor to the next, until at the very last it was given to a young movie producer in Hollywood, along with the yellowed parchment note that said, "I made this for ye in mine grand dame's favourite manner. May ye be of goode cheere upon this, the Holiest of Days!"

The movie producer, who prided himself on always recognizing a piece of dreck when he saw it, took one whiff of the mummified fruitcake and said, "This stinks!" and hurled it into his wastebasket.

The fruitcake made it to a landfill, where not a fly dared land upon it.

And yet, upon that very night, a miracle occurred in the fruitcake. You see, it had a bit of dried fig in it, and a few days earlier the fig had spontaneously formed a young maggot, just as in Aristotle's day . . .

The maggot had grown enormous and bloated, and eventually a shell hardened around it as it reached the pupa phase of its existence.

That night, while Benjamin Ravenspell dared dream of fame and sat with his mouse friends scarfing down pizza, the hardened crust of the pupa shattered.

That night, while reporters gathered around Ben's house, something odd emerged—a fly as large as a crow.

It crept out of its shell and spent long moments just shivering, silently regarding the cold stars above and the lights of jet planes that roared overhead.

It climbed to the top of a junk pile, making its way over a patch of dried roses and through the remains of a broken television. As it dragged itself up the pile, it stopped to collect odd items along the way: a tube of used lipstick, some old enamel paint, a bit of eyeliner, and a child's charm bracelet.

At last its bloated body came to rest upon the ruins of an old fishing boat, one that seemed now to be sailing upon a sea of rubbish.

There the fly sat, quivering, and shaking its wings as they began to harden.

She was a huge fly, and in the cool starlight she cast a terrifying spell. She took all of her youth and bestowed it upon the bracelet, so that she could always keep it with her.

The bracelet was white, with odd little things—plastic four-leafed clovers, sailing ships, and bears' teeth—dangling from it. She put the bracelet around her neck, the elastic pulled tight.

Afterward, she used a bit of burnished chrome as a mirror and began to apply the make-up.

The great fly was a bright iridescent green in color, and its faceted red eyes shone like rubies.

A little eyeliner helped bring out the color of those eyes, making them as red as blood.

The sensory hairs around her mandibles stood up like horns. She used mascara to thicken these.

The old model paints added a little blush to her cheeks.

She sat for long moments, admiring herself in the mirror and enjoying her first taste of fresh air.

But with the rising of the sun, she stood on the bow of the boat and called out, "Arise, my people! Waken from your deathly slumber. Break the shells that bind you. The End of Time is upon us, when all of the world shall wonder and despair!"

The fly crouched for a long moment, waiting for a response, and then the entire landfill began to shudder and seethe. Everywhere, as far as her multifaceted eyes could see, flies began to rise to her call—hatching from rotting burritos, climbing out of old tin cans, struggling up from all of the stink and sewage left by mankind.

There were trillions of them, flies of every kind—horseflies and bluebottle flies, houseflies and sand flies, white flies and fruit flies.

The morning suddenly began to buzz as if in anticipation, for the wings of flies hummed incessantly.

"I am Belle Z. Bug, Lord of the Flies," the monster fly roared. "The end of all who oppose us is at hand. The heavens shall be our throne, and the earth shall be our footstool!"

CHAPTER 4

THE TOAD WARRIOR

Armed with sharp claws, rows of teeth, and poisonous skin, the African cane toad is the most vicious member of the toad family and is almost impossible to get rid of.

Yet it has become a favorite of sugar cane farmers around the world, and farmers have introduced it in the Americas and Australia, for it is the only animal known to eat the voracious cane rat, which has been known to devastate entire fields of sugar cane.

The largest known cane toad was found in Australia. Weighing nearly twenty-four pounds, the locals nicknamed it "Toad-zilla"!
—FROM THE RAVENSPELL COOL BESTIARY

It is a well-known fact that Oregon is one of the rainiest states in all of North America. In fact, it is said that people in Oregon never get a suntan—instead they just rust.

But what is not so well known is that the state has a small desert smack dab in the middle of its wettest rainforest, up near Dallas, Oregon. The desert is very small indeed—only about the width of an umbrella. Nevertheless, while the rest of Oregon floods each winter, this desert has gone over two hundred years without getting blessed by a single drop of rain.

It is called Dinky Desert, and Oregon's Bureau of Oddities considers it to be one of the state's greatest treasures—right up there with the Monroe Bigfoot Wildlife Refuge, where one can go to see thousands of wild bigfoots out in forests dining on fern sprouts, salmon berries, and often shaking down campers for Twinkies.

Dinky Desert has been measured and studied by scientists for years. There are no trees above it to give it shelter, no mountains or rocks nearby to keep it dry. Indeed, many a scientist has gone out during fierce thunderstorms and used lasers to verify that while the rest of the ground around the desert got drenched, not a single raindrop landed on Dinky Desert.

Back in the 1940s, Albert Einstein himself was hired to figure out the odds that every single raindrop falling for two hundred years would somehow miss that spot, and he found the odds so difficult to calculate that he developed a severe cramp in the left temporal lobe of his brain that bothered him until his dying day, giving him nervous twinges.

Ultrasound scans of the sands beneath the desert, taken in 1989, revealed a single curiosity—the bones of some very large toads.

The desert itself is surrounded by a chain-link fence, provided by Oregon's Bureau of Oddities, who thoughtfully provided a sign declaring the desert a state monument. Unfortunately, the marsh grass, cattails, and wild blue mountain iris-es that surround the desert grow so tall that no one can see the sign.

So it was that that night, under the cool light of ten thousand stars, a shadow took shape above the Dinky Desert. It was a shadow shaped like a tall man who wore a black robe that swept to the ground. His deep hood covered his face, but his skeletal hands poked out of the ends of his long robes. He raised a finger that was nothing but bone, and a hissing voice whispered, "Arise, O wind! May the heavens shake and thunder. Awaken, O my foul servants!"

With that, a small storm arose. It was very tiny indeed, about four feet across, and weather track-ers who saw it on radar imagined that it was only a lonely goose flying through the night.

Yet the clouds roared over the fields and woods, thundering and shaking, and then the storm parked above the Dinky Desert, some thirty feet off the ground, where blue lightning flashed and struck the earth, blackening huge patches of grass.

Rain poured down fiercely, a deluge!

As the sand turned to mud, something strange happened.

Three giant toads came to life!

It wasn't that the toads were dead at all. They were *estivating*. Just as a bear will go to sleep and hibernate during the winter, certain animals can go to sleep during dry spells. Some toads, lizards, and fish burrow down into the sand or mud, let their bodies dry up, and shrink down to nothing but skin and bones.

But when the rain falls again, these animals can soak up water like a sponge, then dig their way up to feed.

Thus, our toads awoke, and that night they scrabbled and shoved their massive red bodies out of the sand and sat in the storm.

"We have awakened," one toad said, his croak more hoarse than usual. "How long has it been this time? How long?"

His name was Maximus, for he was the largest toad on earth. But the others just called him Max for short. Max the Toad Warrior.

The other two toads merely grunted in wonder. They were too weak to think well yet.

"It has been long ages—" the shadow hissed, "too long! Goodness and joy have overtaken the earth, and the world grows fat and lazy.

"The time has come for me to be reborn, for the Ever Shade to take a new form. You, Maximus, must gather my armies in preparation for the End of Time."

"How long, O my master?" Max begged, blinking his eyes to a close and lowering his fat red snout to the ground.

"No one must know the hour or place of my return," Ever Shade whispered, "for I have enemies who would try to stop me. Rest assured that it will be soon!"

With that, Ever Shade looked up at the stars and reached out a long, bony hand. He drew back his hood to reveal the horror of his face—a grinning skull that glowed faintly, with only a thin layer of greenish flesh covering it. He had holes for eyes.

Reaching for the stars, he made a clawing motion, as if to gather them. "Not only the earth," he said. "This time I shall have the stars, too!"

With that, he began to fade until only darkness remained.

A terrible hunger assailed Max as he stared at the place where his master had disappeared, and he knew from past experience that he must have slept for years. He was feeble from starvation.

Now, Max was not your common cane toad. He was a sorcerer—a powerful one—and he only woke when his evil master needed him.

He could sense evil—feel it rising—and he longed to see his master's face again. Max could not luxuriate in the rain for long. He needed to prepare for the war to come.

He hopped out of the desert, his massive red body surging with every leap, then landing like strawberry Jell-O with every heavy plop.

His honor guards followed.

Along the way, he found a rusty old spike that he thought he could use as a weapon.

It was near dawn when he reached the highway. The sun was a beautiful pink ball rising over the Cascade Mountain range, and the fields all around, planted in rye grass, were emerald green. Canada geese honked as they flew overhead on a cool wind.

He peered at farmhouses in the distance, the black-and-white cows in their fences, and thought, *Much has changed since last I awoke.*

Years ago he had seen Indian villages with their lodge houses here. Instead of cattle, there had been elk and moose roaming the valley.

Max hopped out of the grass and across a strip of gravel, finding something strange—a great barren patch of black trail covered with bits of gravel and tar. The trail stretched as far as the toad could see in either direction, with thin, white stripes running down the middle.

"What's this?" one of the guards, Caesar, asked. "It looks like a trail of some sort, but even a mammoth doesn't walk on trails this wide—and it's been awhile since we've seen one of those."

The toads sat, pondering the trail.

Who could have made this and for what purpose? they wondered.

It was early morning still, and a bee flew over Max's head. He considered zapping it with his tongue, but he didn't have a taste for honey-flavored stingers this morning.

Suddenly, down the blacktopped trail, he saw a beast coming. It made a blaring sound, like some enormous goose . . .

* * *

Freeway Freddy was carrying a heavy load in his big-rig truck that morning—several tons of prime baker's potatoes out of Idaho—and he had no time to slow down for some silly animals.

He spotted the giant toads squatting on Highway 99 from nearly a mile away and blasted his horn. The toads didn't move, so he chuckled to himself, "Mornin' there, roadkill. Looks like you're all on the highway to heaven."

Freeway Freddy had given the toads fair warning. He made it a point to give every animal a fair warning before he ran it over.

He certainly wasn't going to stop. He had to get his potatoes to market before they rotted or began to sprout.

So he floored the gas and barreled on . . .

* * *

Max the Toad Warrior stared death in the face. The truck came grumbling toward him like an enraged buffalo, the ground rumbling beneath Max's toes.

"Uh, sir," Caesar said, "I think that monster means to kill us."

"The intent is mutual," Max said.

With that, the honor guards both took mighty hops, landing on opposite sides of the highway, leaving the Toad Warrior to his own devices . . .

* * *

Freeway Freddy chortled with glee and grabbed his CB radio. "Breaker, breaker, good buddies," he shouted into the mike. "Anyone out there in the mood for frog legs? I'm bout to flatten the fattest ol' bullfrog you ever did see!"

The big rig thundered over the highway, draw-ing closer to the doomed toad. It was a huge crea-ture, a reddish color that Freddy had never seen before, with golden eyes like the devil.

But what's that in its paws? Freddy wondered.

He peered down as he neared. The giant frog seemed to be holding something up in its paws. It had a stick or something, and it was waving it like a little sword.

"Well, I'll be!" Freddy said in amazement as he hit the frog . . .

* * *

Max the Toad Warrior braced for impact with the giant truck. Just before it hit, he cast a small spell—one that gave him supernatural strength and made his bones harder than titanium.

Then Max threw himself against the front tire, stabbing it and pushing upward at the same instant . . .

* * *

The big rig truck reacted as if it had just hit a rock wall. The cab exploded upward, throwing Freeway Freddy a dozen feet in the air. The air bag deployed in his face, and Freddy couldn't see a blasted thing for a moment.

Then the trailer behind him tipped, and the whole vehicle flipped on its side and went sliding down the freeway in a rain of splintering windshield, with the screams and groans of tortured metal.

When the truck finally ground to a halt, Freddy could see over the top of the air bag just enough to spot dozens of potatoes rolling along the highway, carried by the force of the crash.

Over the CB radio, some trucker with a thick southern accent said, "Ten-four, good buddy. That's a pository on them frog legs. I'd be glad to have 'em. Them's good eatin'!"

* * *

On the freeway, the three toads gathered into a small knot and surveyed the damage. The truck that had tried to run them over was lying on its side in ruin. The trailer had ripped open, spilling potatoes everywhere. The smell of diesel fuel filled the morning air.

Now the driver came crawling out the side window, shouting in wonder and alarm. He bounded to the ground and went racing away.

The three toads eyed him, and Max grinned in satisfaction.

The thing that attacked me wasn't an animal at all, he realized. *It's a machine!*

A fly came buzzing overhead, perhaps ten feet in the air. A normal toad would never have had a chance to catch it, but the Toad Warrior was far from normal.

He hopped eight feet up, zapped his sticky tongue out, expertly caught the fly on its tip, and then did a back flip as he landed perfectly on all fours.

The other toads gazed at him in admiration. "I love the taste of flies in the morning," Caesar said softly.

Max rolled the dead fly around on his tongue, considering. The world had changed much since last he had awakened. There were strange new trails, new inhabitants in the land, and monsters beyond his imagination.

But the fly still tasted as sweet as ever.

"Yes," the Toad Warrior agreed thoughtfully, "it tastes . . . like victory!"

CHAPTER 5

DAY OF THE PAPARAZZI

". . . everyone will be famous for fifteen minutes."
—ANDY WARHOL

Benjamin Ravenspell woke that morning feeling anxious. He hadn't slept well that night. Oh, it was great sleeping in his own bed again—even if it was the size of a football field. It was even better because he got to have his mouse friends for a sleepover. They were still lying on the bed with him, about fifty of them.

But he'd been troubled by strange dreams during the night.

He'd dreamt that he was in his bedroom when he heard his mother's old bamboo wind chimes clacking together out in the backyard. He'd thought that it was odd, because his mother had thrown them away years ago.

So he'd gotten out of bed, curious. When he did, the night was dark. Clouds raced across the sky. For a brief moment, he saw the wan outline of the moon overhead, and then a cloud blew in front of it, plunging the world into deepest night.

The bamboo wind chimes were still clacking, but it seemed that they were not down by the front porch. Instead, they were clacking out in the trees behind the house. It sounded as if they were moving, as if someone was carrying them away.

A *thief is stealing my mom's wind chimes!* Ben thought.

He ran outside to stop the crook and raced into the backyard.

He heard the clacking under the pine tree and shouted, "Hey, you! What do you think you're doing?"

Just then, the clouds blew away from the moon, and in a sudden beam of light, Ben saw something: a hooded figure walking toward him— a figure whose hands were nothing but bones.

He heard the clacking and realized that it was not wind chimes at all—it was the creature's bones rattling together.

The creature peered at him, and Ben saw the dark hollows of its eyes. It pulled back its hood, revealing a fearsome skull. The skeletal monster spoke, answering his question. "I am coming for you!"

* * *

The dream had wakened Ben, leaving his mouth dry and his heart pounding. For a long hour he'd stayed awake, terrified that he might hear bones clacking in the woods.

After a bit, he heard Amber whine in her sleep. He turned toward her and saw her little feet kicking as if she was running. "Ben, don't leave me!" she said. "You can't leave. I'll die without you!"

She whimpered and kept on running. Ben lay beside her and wanted to comfort her. She was caught in her own nightmare, he realized. Unfortunately, when she woke up, the nightmare wouldn't end.

He considered whispering into her ear, trying to comfort her, but he couldn't promise to come with her, not even in her sleep.

So he lay down and put a paw on her neck, then stroked her gently. "I'm here now," he whispered. "I'm here now, and that is all that matters."

With the coming of day, he felt better, if not completely refreshed. The morning sun was up, shining through the gauzy white curtains of his room.

He heard a strange noise above the house. For an instant it sounded as if a helicopter was hovering overhead, and then the sound faded, then it returned again, then faded, then returned. It was very strange.

He leapt up onto the windowsill and spread the curtains. At that instant, a million lights went off. It was as bright as a nuclear bomb outside! Cameras began flashing everywhere.

Ben shaded his eyes with a paw and peered out the window. His entire backyard was filled with paparazzi—photo-journalists, reporters, news anchors. People began screaming, "Look! There's a mouse in the window!" "Is it Amber?" "Is it Ben?"

But there were more than just reporters outside. Ben saw dozens of groupies, too. There were cute girls carrying signs that said, "We love Ben," while others wore T-shirts that shouted, "Free the mice!"

Overhead, he heard that whirring sound again, and he looked up. Panic took him.

"Dad!" Ben screamed. "There's a stealth helicopter hovering over our house!"

At that instant, a man in black peered from the open door of his helicopter and shouted, "Go! Go! Go!" Instantly, a bunch of other men wearing back leapt out of the helicopter and began slithering down long ropes toward the front door. One of the men had a very large gift basket.

"Dad!" Ben screamed. "There's a bunch of black-ops CIA agents coming to our door bearing gifts!"

Instantly the doorbell rang.

Ben leapt down from the windowsill and raced for the front door. His screams had had little effect on his parents. He was only a mouse, after all, and he could only shout in mouse-sized squeaks.

So Ben ran to the front door and then had to just sit there, staring at it, because he could not open it. Fortunately the doorbell itself woke Ben's dad, who got up groggily and went to the door in his underwear. He opened it just a tad and peeked out.

The black-ops CIA agents all stood on the porch grinning, while ten thousand paparazzi began flashing photographs of his dad's World Wrestling Federation boxer shorts.

"Good morning, Mr. Ravenspell," one of the CIA agents shouted. "I have a gift basket here, compliments of the president of the United States and your friendly neighborhood CIA. I *strongly* advise that you take it."

The agent shoved the basket into his dad's hands, and just for effect, he opened the lapel of his jacket widely enough so that Ben could see a small machine gun—an UZI—with a big silencer on it. The CIA agent flashed a smile and said, "The gifts are for Amber and Ben."

Butch Ravenspell smiled nervously and tried to shut the door, but suddenly some reporter with legs about ten feet long shoved his foot in the crack.

There were confused shouts from the reporters. "Is it true that Amber intends to turn *everyone* in the world into mice?" one reporter cried. Before Ben could deny the accusation, another woman said, "Is it true that Amber has fleas?" A third shouted at Ben, "Do you and Amber really want to get married?"

Ben was about to answer some questions when his dad shouted, "Ben will hold a press conference with the first reporter who hands him a suitcase with one million dollars in it!"

Then he slammed the door. Butch stood for a moment, grinning. "That ought to hold them for a while!" He set the huge gift basket on the floor. Inside was an assortment of cheeses, breads, and fruit juices—all covered with cellophane in the colors of the American flag. A Mylar-covered helium balloon was tied onto the bag and hovered overhead. On one side of the balloon was the gold-colored seal of the president of the United States. On the other side of the balloon was a picture of a CIA agent holding a smoking gun next to his face, sort of like a James Bond poster. Underneath the picture was the slogan, "Your friendly neighborhood CIA!"

Someone rang the doorbell. Butch rolled his eyes and said, "Now what?"

Butch opened the door a crack.

Ben could see the CIA agents slithering back up the ropes into their helicopter. Four reporters stood at the door, each fighting to shove his or her own suitcase through first. "I've got dibs!" one announcer from *60 Minutes* shouted.

Butch grinned at Ben and opened the door just wide enough so that the reporters could push their suitcases in.

"Ben," his dad said, "go tell your mouse friends to start packing their bags. We're going to Disneyland!"

CHAPTER 6

THE MILLIONAIRE
MOUSE CLUB

*Those who say that money can't buy happiness probably
didn't spend enough to really find out.*
—Butch Ravenspell

Amber could not help but feel fretful that morning as the mice prepared for their trip.

In part, it was because she was a mouse. Life is
dangerous when you're down at the bottom of the
food chain, and she was always worried about
something.

They were going to Disneyland, a "play-
ground" that Ben assured her would be lots of fun.
She imagined that maybe the humans would have
some huge wheel that they could all run around
on, or maybe some large plastic tubes to run
through, like the fancy toys that the spotted mice
used to play with at the pet shop, but Ben assured
her, "It's a lot cooler than that. There are really

47

neat rides to go on—like roller coasters and space rides!"

But even though they were supposedly going to have fun, the true reason for the trip weighed heavily on Amber's mind. The black lotus had bloomed, and a great enemy was rising somewhere in the world.

"Shouldn't we do something about it?" Amber asked Lady Blackpool over breakfast. "I mean, shouldn't we go look into the eyes of a newt, or cast a spell at a magic pool, or do *something*—just to find out what kind of monster we're up against?"

The mice were up on the table, eating bread and cheese from a basket. Ben himself was sitting in the front room, being interviewed by some famous morning talk-show host. Bright lights were shining on him, and camera crews took up most of the room.

Huge humans were tromping all over the place. The front room was no place for a mouse.

Lady Blackpool had her own breakfast. Ben's mom had given her a little lunchmeat to nibble on. She looked up with her mouth full of pickle loaf. "Just because you need to know something doesn't mean that you have to cast a spell every time. You need to learn to conserve your magical energy, young lady. Years ago, I cast one spell to handle the problem. Now, every time I need vital information, someone tells me."

"Who tells you?" Amber asked.

"Whoever happens to know," Lady Blackpool said. "They just feel a strange impulse to come and talk to me—the way Rufus Flycatcher did when he told me to come find you."

"Oh," Amber said, still worried. "So someone will come tell us who our enemy is?"

"Yes," Lady Blackpool said, her mouth full.

"When?" Amber asked.

"When I *need* to know," Lady Blackpool said. "So you see, the problem has been solved. One little wish made long ago, and I don't have to go running around hunting for newts or asking spiders to send messages over the worldwide web."

Amber was just beginning to realize that there were all kinds of ways to communicate. Sure, she could look into a newt's eye in order to see a vision of the future, or she could ask a spider to send a message. But Ben had told her that humans had a web, too, and television and telephones.

Amber sat nibbling on a bit of rye bread for a moment. A reporter was interviewing Ben, and Amber's ears perked up.

"So, Ben," the woman asked, "tell me, what's the best part of being a mouse?"

"Uh, I don't know," Ben said.

"Well, do you like the food?"

Ben shook his head sadly. "Not really. There's nothing much to eat but grain and stuff. It's like eating granola all the time. And, the worst part is, other animals are always trying to eat you!"

"But there must be something fun about being a mouse?"

"Well, I can jump so high that I feel like Superman," Ben said.

"Are you angry that Amber turned you into a mouse?"

"I was at first," Ben said, "but she didn't do it on purpose. I was trying to feed her to a friend's lizard, and . . . and it just sort of happened. It's not like she's evil or anything. She's not like Nightwing the Bat, or the Wizard of Ooze!"

"I understand that you've had some grand adventures," the reporter said. "We'll come back to those later.

"Right now I have another question: do you look forward to the day when you're human again?"

Amber sat with bated breath. She wanted Ben to say no. She wanted him to stay with her forever. It wasn't just that he was the handsomest mouse she'd ever seen. Without him, she'd be almost powerless. She needed Ben to stay with her. The *world* needed Ben to stay with her if she was going to fight the Ever Shade. Surely he had to see that!

But Ben answered, "Oh, man, I can hardly wait to be human again! I mean, there's all kinds of things that I want to do: ride my skateboard, go to the mall . . ."

Amber's heart broke. Certainly there had to be things he liked about being a mouse.

"Are you worried about how things might change once you turn back into a human?" the reporter asked.

"Yeah," Ben said. "Mice grow old fast. Every week for a mouse is like a year to a human. So I figure that when I turn back into a boy, I'm going to look two years older. I'll look like a twelve-year-old. I might even have hair under my armpits!"

The reporter chuckled. "I wasn't thinking about that; I was thinking about the fame. You'll be famous now—the most famous boy in the world. You won't be able to go outside without drawing a crowd."

"Yeah, I guess I am kinda worried about that," Ben admitted.

Then the topic turned to Nightwing the Bat, and Amber quit listening. She hopped about in the gift basket, searching for something new to eat.

The cheeses came in several different colors and varieties. Amber enjoyed tasting the exotic flavors. But as she peered in, she noticed something strange. There was a very small red thing in the basket, just the right size for her paw. She recognized it immediately. Ben's dad had been using one earlier. It was a telephone. But this one was tiny—just the right size for a mouse.

She picked it up and studied it. Ben's phone had lots of buttons on it. This had only one. She pushed the button, just the way Butch had done.

"Hel-looooo," a human crooned sweetly. "Who do I have the pleasure of speaking to?"

Amber stood for a moment, feeling both excited and rather baffled. She'd never had her own phone before. She wasn't quite sure how to use it.

"Uh, this is Amber, uh, the wizard . . . uh, mouse. I mean the mouse wizard."

"Good morning, Amber," the voice said. "It's so nice to hear from you. I hope you're enjoying my little gift basket."

"Oh, it's really nice!" Amber enthused. "There's all kinds of yummy cheese!"

"*American* cheese," the fellow corrected. "So, Amber, there's something I've been wondering. Are you a Republican," he said sweetly, "or a *Democrat?*"

"I'm a mouse—" she said, feeling rather baffled, "a feeder mouse!"

There was a long pause.

"What's a feeder mouse?" the man asked, a bit perplexed.

"A mouse that's raised in pet shops," Amber said, "so that kids can feed them to their snakes and lizards."

"Well," the fellow said, "we'll put an end to that. The president is pushing a bill through this morning, calling for an end to such . . . such barbarism!"

That sounded good to Amber. "Okay. Who are you?"

The fellow hesitated then answered, "Let's just say that I'm a friend . . . a very powerful and influential friend. That's what I do in life. I make friends . . . with other powerful people." He halted a moment, as if to let Amber ponder what that might mean.

"Actually," the man went on, "you could be a big help to us. You see, we're going to need an emissary . . . someone on the payroll . . . an *ambassador*.

This mouse would sort of help our beloved country develop official diplomatic ties to mousedom. Would *you* be willing to help?"

Amber was all for saving mice. "Okay."

"Great! Wonderful!" the fellow said, evidently very pleased. "We'll announce the appointment today. We need to talk about a salary, of course."

"Celery?" Amber asked. Ben's mom had given her a piece last night. It had an interesting taste.

"A salary," the man corrected. "You know, *money?*"

Amber had heard all about money, of course. Ben's mom and dad were collecting suitcases full of it. Already they had four, each with one million dollars in it. That's why Ben had to do the interviews. Apparently, humans had to work for money, and Ben was working. Amber was delighted to learn that she might get a suitcase full of money, too. Ben told her that she could trade money for all kinds of things—pizza, vegetables, houses.

"Oh," Amber cried in delight. "Do I get a million dollars?!"

The fellow sort of coughed. "Well, uh, if that's what you want . . ."

"Yes, please, in a pretty suitcase—with . . . with flowers on it!"

The man was silent for a moment. "I suppose, uh, that you'll want this *under* the table?"

Amber looked down from the table. She figured that one of those big suitcases was going to be awfully hard to move, and she certainly didn't want it way up here *on* the table. "Yes, under the table would be perfect!"

"One last thing," the man said. "I understand that you've created a sort of a haven for mice out there in Oregon, a place where they can live in safety and freedom. Have you considered what you will call it?"

"Yes," Amber said happily. "Meadowsweet picked out a name for it just a while ago. We're going to call it 'Mouse-atopia!'"

"Wonderful!" the fellow said in a smiling voice. "I like that name. Well, I'm sure that you'll be in touch. Feel free to call me anytime."

He hung up, and Amber sat there for a long minute. The phone began to make a buzzing noise, and she asked, "Are you still there? What's that noise?" But the fellow didn't answer.

Ben had just finished with his interview, so Amber went to him. She didn't have anything to say. She just wanted to be with him. In the past two weeks, he'd become her best friend. She hated the thought that he might leave her soon.

Ben was sweating dangerously when she found him. Mice cannot cope with heat very well, and the harsh lights from the camera had left Ben shivering. Water droplets filled his fur, and he was preening in vain, trying to get rid of them lest he catch a chill.

Amber stayed with him for a long moment, to make sure he would be all right. She said nothing, just sat gazing at him steadily.

He finished preening and studied her in silence for a minute.

"I'll miss you when I go to S.W.A.R.M.," Amber said at last. "Somehow, it won't feel right without you."

Ben didn't speak for a moment. "I'm sorry that I can't go with you."

"*Can't* go or won't?" Amber demanded.

"I kept my part of the bargain," Ben said. "I helped save all of the mice in the world—more than you ever imagined."

Amber looked for an argument that might change his mind, and she found one easily enough. "But that was before we knew about the Ever Shade! Now everything is changed. Now it isn't just the mice that need saving—it's the whole world. It's mice and bears and people, too. Your mom and dad might need saving—even you!"

"I know that," Ben said. "Don't you think I know that? I've been thinking about that all night."

"You don't like me, is that it?" Amber demanded.

Ben hesitated. "I like you, Amber," he said at last. "I've always liked you. I just don't like being a mouse."

Ben crept close to her, looked into her eyes, and reached up with one paw. He petted her face, bringing his paw down from her ear and along her cheek bone. "I really do like you, Amber."

She'd never enjoyed the touch of another mouse so much, and she sat for a moment, just weeping. Ben thought that she wept in relief because he liked her, but Amber wept because she knew that she had to go away, and she would have to go without him.

* * *

Sixty minutes later, a man came to the door with a gift for Amber—a suitcase with flowers on it!

Amber was disappointed when Ben's dad popped open the suitcases filled with money. Amber hadn't really had any idea what money would look like. It was just a bunch of scraps of paper, all stacked nicely, but all with pictures of the same dead guy on them.

"So, uh, what's so neat about money again?" Amber asked.

"Everything!" Butch confirmed. "You can buy things with it. You can buy pizzas and houses. You can travel the world! Now, where did you get this again?"

"Can you buy mice?" Amber asked. A worry had been nagging her ever since last night. Some people in the world were all for freeing the mice. Other folks were against the idea.

"Of course you can, dear," Ben's mom answered. The whole family was hovering around the suitcases, staring at the money, along with Amber's friends.

"How many could we buy?" Amber asked.

"Well," Ben's mom admitted, "I paid half a dollar for you. At that price, we could buy two million mice with each suitcase."

"Wow!" Ben said. "That's a lot of mice!"

Ben's mom, Mona, nodded, and her eyes kind of misted over. "Then I think that's what we should do with this money," she said. She leaned over and clicked the suitcases shut.

Amber hadn't known what to think of Mona. Amber had never imagined actually liking a human before, or having one as a friend. Mona had once sucked Amber up with a vacuum cleaner and thrown her in the garbage can.

But at that instant everything changed. Amber's heart pounded as it broke.

She's giving me millions of dollars, Amber realized. *She's giving freedom to my people*.

"You're going to help the mice?" Amber asked in surprise, just to make sure that she'd heard correctly.

Ben's mom nodded. "I think that it's the least I can do."

Amber tried to figure out what she meant. The least she could do would have been nothing. She was doing a lot more than that.

Tears of gratitude filled Amber's eyes. For the second time that day, she found herself feeling weepy over some human.

"I want to thank you for bringing my son back to me," Mona explained. "You don't know how much it hurts to lose someone forever, and you don't know how happy I feel knowing that he's alive."

Amber knew what it felt like to lose someone. She had lost her mother in the pet shop. Amber's mom was a feeder mouse, the lowest kind of mouse, the kind that children bought to feed to snakes and lizards. Reason told Amber that her mother was gone forever.

But Amber had to hope that, like Barley Beard, her mother had been purchased by some children who wanted a pet. Maybe like Barley Beard, Amber's mom would escape—or better yet, her captors would set her free.

Amber knew in some small part how Ben's mom must feel right now. Mona Ravenspell had lost her son, and Amber had brought him back to her.

Ben's mom leaned down on the floor and tenderly stroked Amber's back. Then Mona kissed Amber on the snout.

Amber felt astonished by this sign of affection from someone who had once been an enemy. Mona Ravenspell—freeing the mice.

Amber decided that she liked Mona. She felt genuinely grateful. But Amber could not afford to like her too much.

She thinks I'm going to turn Ben back into a human soon, Amber realized. *She thinks we'll be friends.*

I hate having to break her heart!

CHAPTER 7

EVIL FOMENTING

I don't want to just rule the world. I want to do it with style.
—BELLE Z. BUG

The brain of a fly is vastly superior to that of a human. That is why, for example, a newborn fly can easily walk around on six legs, while a newborn human can't even manage two. And, of course, flies can easily pick locks and enter houses quietly, even though humans do their best to keep them out.

But though the *quality* of a fly's brain is phenomenal, most flies have only a very small *quantity* of brain in their heads. In order to be able to fly, they only get a speck of it—just enough to fit on the head of a pin.

But Belle Z. Bug, Lord of the Flies, happened to be born with a massive brain that had more analytical power than a Cray supercomputer.

Belle had grown to be the size of a beagle, and so the superior nature of her brain made her a genius of unimaginable proportions.

Much to Belle's delight, she had discovered upon hatching that she was born with a built-in HD television receiver in her head. All she had to do to watch TV was move her antennae around just so, and she could switch channels with ease. The television pictures flashed with magnificent clarity upon all ten thousand facets in her eyes.

Thus, as she had crawled from her place of birth, her mummified fruitcake, she had learned to speak English. From various movies she had also seen how advanced human civilization was.

Just as quickly, she devised a plan to destroy it.

Within minutes of birth, she surveyed her foul empire—the Los Angeles City dump—watching the sun rise over the dump with her natural eyes while her inner eyes switched from one television station to the next.

Below her, a great army of flies was hatching, flies as far as the eye could see. She had commanded them to hatch from their hardened shells, and spurred on by her magic powers, they had hatched by the trillions. But one question remained: would they follow her?

One of them called out, "So, uh, tell us why we should serve you."

Belle Z. Bug knew that this was a delicate moment. She had to convert these flies to evil, and her schedule required that it be done quickly.

So she settled on a scheme—one she had

picked up on from the humans on television, a nefarious scheme that she learned about on a home-shopping channel.

"Listen, O my people!" Belle cried to be heard above the massive army of winged insects. "I am a fly, just like you. We are flies, and flies are hated by every creature of the field."

Many flies buzzed in agreement at this, for it was obvious that flies were treated unfairly— slapped at or swatted by cattle and humans, eaten by other animals, cursed at and avoided.

"Why are we hated?" Belle Z. Bug demanded.

"Uh, cause we spread plagues?" one housefly hazarded. "Because we bite?" a horsefly shouted. "Could you repeat the question?" someone farther back in the crowd asked.

"We are hated," Belle Z. Bug answered thunderously, "because, *we are ugly!*"

The flies that covered the land quit buzzing. Their wings drooped in despair, and some of them openly wept. It was a cruel truth. The flies knew they were ugly. But there was nothing they could do about it.

"The great creator," Belle Z. Bug shouted, "the great Master of Field and Fen, *made* us ugly."

She let her words hang over the crowd like a death sentence; the sounds of sobs, the wails of despair, rang out from everywhere.

"But I," Belle shouted, "I have a *cure* for ugliness!"

When the sobs stopped, a trillion flies fell profoundly silent as they peered up at Belle, wondering what she meant.

At that moment, she stood on her back legs and held up various products garnered from the trash pile.

"Here in this hand," she called, "I have fly-liner, to put around your eyes. A small, dark circle will make your many facets shine all that much brighter!"

The flies buzzed in excitement, but not all were convinced. "And here I have fly-shadow, to darken your faces!"

She held up a little tube of clear gel, which humans used as lip balm. "Here I have wing wax, so that your wings will sparkle like garnets in the morning sun." Last of all, she displayed a tube of bright pink paint. "And in this fourth hand, I have carapace color, to make even the roses envy your hue!"

The flies all gaped at her in stunned silence. "Use these products," Belle told them, "and you will be more beautiful! Use enough of my products, and you can be the most beautiful flies in the world!"

There were gasps of wonder and delight from the flies.

But not all were so sure. One fly shouted at Belle, "Are you telling me that if we use your products, other animals will like us?"

Belle didn't hesitate to answer. "I am telling you that they will like you *better*. You will dazzle and delight those who once hated you. You will be invited to picnics. Those who once tried to drive you away will now crave your friendship and stare agog at your magnificent beauty! The world will learn to love flies!"

Her detractor seemed unconvinced, and to be honest, Belle didn't believe it either. So she added, "More importantly, any fly that does not use my products will be seen for what they are— ugly." She stood up and shouted urgently, "Think about it. How could you—how could any of you— hope to find a mate if you are uglier than your neighbor?"

This idea hit the flies like a revelation. They were in a beauty competition!

Many of them surged forward to get the make-up while a few others scouted around amid the trash, looking for some of their own. But Belle raised a hand, warning them to stop.

"Wait!" she cried. "You cannot just *have* fly-shadow. You must *earn* it!"

"How?" someone pleaded.

So Belle Z. Bug outlined her plan. Each fly had to go forth into the earth and tell two other flies about Belle's makeup. Only when they had earned three eager converts could they have some fly-liner. When those three had each gained three converts, a fly could rise to the next level and gain free fly-shadow. As a lucky fly kept moving higher in the plan, rising up to the next tier, he or she would gain greater rewards. With mask-era, a fly could color its face. With Prime Slime, a fly could get great-tasting food that would keep its belly from getting too bloated; next on the list of rewards was Solid Gold Miracle Mold—"eat it once and you'll never grow old!"

The promise of rewards was vast, and many of them sounded too good to be true. But at the very top, at the thirteenth level, Belle's agents could win the ultimate prize—one that would engender envy from every fly in the land: a bright pink coat of carapace color!

The flies cheered to hear the grand news, and immediately a furious buzzing ensued as flies, eager to get in on the rewards, spread the word.

Thus, in a matter of moments, Belle converted a trillion flies to her plan, turning them from mere household pests into her mindless minions.

* * *

As her empire spread that morning, Belle Z. Bug sat in the sun watching *Good Morning America*.

All around Belle, flies were frantically putting on fly-shadow, gossiping, and dreaming of even greater rewards. Belle ignored them as she studied the news.

The humans of the world were all in a frazzle. A mouse had displayed phenomenal magic powers only the night before. Belle watched as Amber transformed nuclear bombs into fireworks and transmogrified a human into a worm.

"Nice bit of work, that," Belle told the flies that swarmed around her. But she also saw how Amber had nearly died from the wizard wearies, and instinctively Belle knew that the mouse was vulnerable . . .

Meanwhile, Belle's power was growing by the moment. She didn't have just one familiar. She had thousands of them secreted among the swarms of flies that surrounded her. They buzzed about, flying from garbage pile to garbage pile, unaware of just how much mage dust they gathered in the process, ignorant of how much power Belle drained from them.

She sat pondering what to do as the sun climbed above the hills. Seagulls flew toward the dump with the coming of the sun, but when they saw that it was covered with flies that buzzed angrily, they retreated.

Shortly after dawn, the first of the city's dump trucks came—huge yellow trucks, piled high with delectable garbage.

The humans came roaring down the road, but as the drivers saw the vast horde of flies covering the dump to a depth of several inches, the trucks ground to a stop.

Belle spotted a human inside the cab of the truck, peering through the windshield, wondering what to do. Suddenly he began to back up.

With a clamor of wings, Belle leapt from her grungy throne and flew to the truck. She smashed through the window and leapt up onto the steering wheel, staring the garbage truck driver in the eye.

"I'll take your garbage," Belle said. "Leave it!"

"Uh, who are you?" the driver asked. He was a dark little Latin American. His nametag said that he was called Emilio. He spoke with a thick accent.

"I am Belle Z. Bug, Lord of the Flies!" Belle exulted. "This dump is mine. All dumps are mine!

I demand tribute! I want more garbage from you—more garbage, do you hear me?"

"Yes, I hear you," Emilio said, shaking. "You want lots more garbage?"

"All of it!" Belle Z. Bug demanded. "I want all of the garbage in the world!"

"Okay," Emilio said, "but I will have to talk to my boss!"

Belle Z. Bug whirled and shouted at her minions. "Seize this shipment! Diapers and rotten burritos go to my royal chambers. Fruit goes to the fruit flies. The rest of this junk is for our armies."

Buzzing in delight, eager to do Belle's will, ten billion flies rose up in a huge black cloud. They descended upon the garbage truck in a droning maelstrom. Thousands of flies attached to each piece of garbage and then strained with effort as they lifted their spoils into the air.

Emilio watched with his jaw open, gazing in dismay. When the flies were done, the demon Belle shouted, "I will expect you back shortly, with more tribute!"

"Whatever," Emilio said. "I'll be coming and going all day!"

He began backing his truck up, muttering under his breath. "The stuff I have to put up with on this job . . . Ay, I should get a raise!"

Belle buzzed off in triumph. Part of her plan was already in play. This first step of her master's bid for global conquest was a success. Belle was taking over the world's dumps. But she knew that she would face opposition.

To the commander of her horseflies, she whispered, "Go now, and bring me Amber the mouse. She must do obeisance before me!"

* * *

Emilio drove off, shaken by his experience. As soon as he got out from under the cloud of flies, he grabbed his two-way radio and called headquarters.

"Senor," he said, "we got big problemas!"

"What kind of problemas?" his boss demanded.

"Giant mutant flies have taken over the garbage dump!"

"Again?" his boss whined. "Just what I need to hear." He fell silent then added, "I'll call county pest control and have them send a crop duster over with some bug spray."

"Forget the crop duster, man," Emilio said. "I'm telling you, you better get Governor Shortzenbeggar down here with a rocket launcher. There's a really big fly!"

CHAPTER 8

MR. TOAD'S WILD RIDE

When you find that you have lost your way in life,
triple your speed. No, it won't help you find yourself, but
it makes being lost a lot more fun!
—RUFUS FLYCATCHER

"Spare me!" a fly cried. "Spare me, I beg of you!"

The fly was stuck to the tongue of Max the Toad Warrior. He held his tongue out as far as possible, offering the fly to a newt.

"Gee, thanks!" the newt cried. Then he lunged forward, grasped the fly, and gulped it down.

The morning was sunny, but the toads had found the newt in some marshy ground, shaded by small oaks. Spring was coming, and all around, tiny yellow daffodils and blue mountain orchids were beginning to rise up from the leaf mold.

The newt perched atop a spotted mushroom and gazed into the distance, allowing the toads to see their future.

"Show me our enemies and my master's true servant," the Toad Warrior whispered.

The golden eyes of the newt grew cloudy, as if a storm suddenly began to brew and roil within them, and then Max saw a distant scene.

A strange young mouse appeared. He had a skull for a face, it seemed, until Max looked more closely. No, it was just a walnut shell carved to look like a skull. The mouse had what might have been a thick piece of spider silk coiled around his shoulder, and he carried a strange something in his paw. It might have been a pine needle, but it was more the color of ice.

No, he decided, *it is made of metal, like the monster that attacked me this morning.*

What strange world have I wakened to? Max wondered. *Mice have begun using tools, and monsters made of metal roam the earth.*

The young mouse was sitting upon the legs of a human woman who wore a sunny dress, and nearby perched a shrew, some voles, and more mice.

The sight of so many mice made Max's stomach grumble with hunger.

Brutus, one of his honor guards, said, "Are you sure this vision isn't showing us our dinner?"

Max ran his tongue over his parched lips. He was a huge toad, a gargantuan toad, and his hunger couldn't be sated by a few flies and potato bugs. He needed meat—lots of it.

"I asked to see our enemies," Max retorted.

"Perhaps," Caesar suggested, "our enemies will *be* our dinner!"

Brutus began laughing, and soon all three toads were giggling at the idea. Then the image of the mice cleared.

The newt's eye went as dark as a thundercloud once again, then something new took form: an image of refuse, garbage—hundreds and hundreds of acres of it—all covered with flies so thick that the entire landscape was black. Flies were crawling atop the backs of flies in a mass of insect flesh several inches deep. Many of the flies were newly hatched, and so they sat in the sun, buzzing and flapping their wings, while others buzzed tentatively in the sky as they took their maiden flights; others were darting about eagerly.

The sound of droning filled the air, becoming deafening.

There, atop the pile of garbage, squatted an enormous green fly, nearly as large as Max himself. The fly stood preening her face with her front feet. Her faceted eyes were so red that they looked like glowing coals, and her iridescent green exoskeleton appeared to be as hard as armor.

The great fly stopped preening and peered down at a scrap of newspaper. It was reading words written by humans. Or perhaps it was merely looking at pictures. Max could see that on the newspaper was the image of mice—the mice he'd just seen in his vision.

Suddenly the monster fly seemed startled.

It raised its head and drew forward so that its face filled the entirety of the newt's eye. Max was

filled with a cold certainty that the monster somehow knew that he was watching.

Only a mage of great power could have known
that he was spying on her.

"Come!" the monster fly whispered. The
words were not spoken. Instead the sound of the
fly's voice penetrated Max's skull, slamming
through flesh and bone like a bullet.

Max grunted and lurched back half a pace,
afraid that this fly would somehow emerge from
the vision.

But nothing more happened.

The newt's eye went cloudy, and then its color
returned: golden flecks among a sea of deep
brown. The newt began strolling away, off to look
for a morning meal.

Max had never seen a fly like the one in his
vision. It was huge, far larger than any insect he'd
ever encountered. Nothing like it had haunted
even his wildest nightmares.

"That's our ally?" Brutus asked.

Max the Toad Warrior whirled and retraced
his path. He would need to gather mage dust if he
was going to confront this magical mouse. The
best way to do that was to travel, keeping low to
the ground.

He found the huge vehicle that he'd fought on
the highway. A few cars filled with people had
gathered nearby, and some of them were studying
the wreck.

Max cast a small spell, then used his might to
push the truck upright. The humans saw him

then. Some screamed and fled into their vehicles. One man came up to Max and tried to stomp on him.

That was a big mistake. Max grabbed the human's foot as it fell, then tossed the man forty feet—over a ditch and into a field.

The rest of the humans fled.

Max leapt ten feet, through the broken windshield, and waited on the dashboard for his comrades to find their own way into the massive machine.

He cast a spell upon the big rig. "Take me to my master's flies . . ."

The truck's engine grumbled and turned over, and in minutes it was roaring down the road, heading south.

Max hopped up onto the seat and used his rear legs to hold himself up. With a mighty effort he grabbed the steering wheel. He took great delight in turning the truck this way and that, swerving all over the road.

For four long hours, Max drove the truck unimpeded until at last he crossed the border from Oregon into California.

There, he passed a police car by the side of the road. A human inside the car spotted him, a large red toad, driving the truck.

Suddenly the small car raced out behind the truck, throwing a cloud of gravel and dust into the air. Lights on top of the car began to flash blue, red, and white. A siren sent out throbbing pulses of sound.

For long minutes the car followed, veering this way and that as the officer tried to get a better look at Max. Soon other police cars joined in, a long line of them—sixteen in all—doing a slow chase down the freeway.

The sight of it was unnerving. The sound of the sirens, their burps and stutters and wails, jarred Max's ears.

"What do you think these humans want?" Brutus asked. "What kinds of weapons do you think they have?"

One police car roared up beside the Toad Warrior. The human driver picked up a megaphone and shouted to Max, "Pull over! We have you surrounded. Pull over now!"

Max cast a spell to let him understand human speech. He looked out the window to the police officer. The man was pale with fear. Apparently the police officer had never done battle with a magic cane toad before.

"Who are you to command the great Toad Warrior!" Max shouted. He spun the wheel, veered into the police car, and sent it hurtling off the road.

"What are you doing?" Brutus cried. "They have us surrounded! You must be mad!"

Max laughed. He slammed on the brakes, and a second police car smashed into the back of the big rig.

That seemed to anger the humans. They began pulling up behind Max's truck, trying to get near. He swerved as he raced down the road, knocking police cars into the ditch one after another.

Suddenly he saw a police car blocking the road just ahead. Its human driver stood off to the side of the road. Max barreled into the car. It exploded into a brilliant fireball, and for a moment all was flame and searing heat as the truck passed through the wreckage.

But the human got his vengeance.

Just as Max passed the policeman, all of the tires on his truck blew. Suddenly he was driving on steel rims. Sparks flew up from the pavement, and the truck made a grinding noise. The vehicle slowed to a crawl, and police cars wailed as they rolled along behind.

Max shook his head sadly.

Ah, he thought, *for the good old days, when I used to ride a mammoth.*

CHAPTER 9

REVELATIONS

*Sometimes, one little piece of knowledge can change
an animal's destiny and shape the world.*
—Rufus Flycatcher

"I think we need to have a little talk," Butch Ravenspell said only a few minutes later. He looked very grim, with his bald head and bulging muscles, and as soon as he spoke, Amber and everyone else scurried to the couch.

He stood for a long minute, looking at Amber's suitcase full of money.

"Now, I want to ask you once again: who gave this to you?"

"Just some man who wanted to be my friend," Amber said.

"A man who wants to be your friend?" Butch said, his tone sounding as if he were disgusted.

Mona chimed in, "Amber, dear, he could be

anyone—a criminal or a drug lord or . . . a crooked politician."

"He says he wants to help the mice," Amber said.

Butch Ravenspell scratched a tattoo on his neck and just grimaced. "Be careful who you choose as friends," he warned. "You never know what they might want from you. It is always best for you to choose them, not let them just choose you. Understand?"

"That is sound advice," Lady Blackpool said.

"Now," Butch Ravenspell said, changing the subject, "I've been thinking about something."

Ben's father knelt down near the couch so that he was so close to the mice that his breath smote Amber like a warm wind. She looked at his handlebar mustache and thought about jumping on it. She imagined that it would be very fun to play on.

"Ben, there is a secret that you should know—a secret that has been in our family for a long, long time. You're not the first one in our family who has been able to gather magical energy. Ravenspell has been our family name for hundreds of years. Once, long ago, there was a sailor in our family who kept a raven as a pet. He carried it around on his shoulder as if it were a parrot, and it is said that he spoke to it, and sometimes the raven would cast magical spells that protected him and brought him riches."

"Cooool!" Ben said, his voice an astonished whisper.

Lady Blackpool nodded her head. "The name of Ravenspell is known among the small fold of

S.W.A.R.M. Arthur Ravenspell was a kind man, the greatest of familiars, and a powerful force for good."

Butch went to the bookcase and pulled down an old volume bound in leather. He opened it to reveal a drawing of a portly man with a doughy face and a cape who had a raven on his shoulder.

"I've never seen that book before," Ben said.

"We kept it out of your reach," Mona replied.

"Before he died," Ben's father said, "Arthur Ravenspell promised that another familiar would someday be born from his line."

Butch pointed to some squiggly black marks on the paper and said, "Here's what he said:

In days of darkness, in a time of death,
Another Ravenspell shall draw his breath.
Here is a sign, for those who can hear:
A nut shall be his helm, a needle his spear.
He shall pull magic from wood and glade.
With a Golden One he'll fight the Ever Shade.

Ben scrunched his nose thoughtfully so that his whiskers wiggled. He was wearing his little nut shell for a help, and he held his needle in his palm.

Amber thought that it was so cool that someone had described him hundreds of years ago.

"Ben," Butch continued, "I first read those words when I was your age, and I thought that our old ancestor had bats in his attic. But now I think that this is serious. Maybe you need to go to this magic school, too."

Ben's whiskers twitched nervously, and he looked up at his father with beady eyes.

"No," Mona said. "I don't want to lose him again. I don't want him to go."

"I don't want him to, either," Butch said. "But maybe it's for the best." He turned to Lady Blackpool. "How dangerous will this school be?"

"Not too dangerous," Lady Blackpool said. "We've been attacked by the students of the Small Animals' Dark Institute of Sorcerous Technology, or S.A.D.I.S.T., but that has not happened for many years."

Amber felt frightened by such news.

Mona began to sob. "It's . . . a nice school, isn't it?"

Lady Blackpool looked around at the house thoughtfully. "It's nice for a school out in the swamps, I suppose. It's nothing like this."

"But it's warm and dry?" Mona begged.

"I'd say more hot and muggy," Lady Blackpool answered. "It's a fine place if you're a water scorpion or a salamander, but the truth is that it's none too pleasant for mammals."

Ben looked frantic. He shouted, "I don't want to go! I want to go to Disneyland, Dad. You promised!"

Amber's heart raced. She wanted him to come so badly.

"There is no reason you can't do both," Lady Blackpool said. "Amber needs mage dust to recharge her magical power. She needs to wander around for a few days, let it collect. You could do that at your Disneyland as well as anywhere else."

"But, I don't want to go to that school," Ben objected. "I mean, what would I do all day—just stand around like I was a stupid battery while Amber used up any mage dust that I collected?"

Everyone looked to Lady Blackpool. The little shrew drew herself up so that the white fur beneath her pointy nose was displayed prominently. "Your schooling will not be easy," she warned. "There is an art to being a great familiar—an art that requires more courage and cunning than you can ever guess."

She paused, and the world seemed silent. Amber suddenly thought that she heard sounds of battle in the distance, as if in a dream. There were shrieks of pain and shouts of fear and a hissing as if an army of kittens were on the prowl. The room seemed to grow dark, and suddenly the only light seemed to be coming from Ben.

Lady Blackpool has cast a spell, Amber realized.

"Ben," the old shrew whispered, seeming to shrink in on herself. "There are prophecies of a golden mouse that will come to save the world through the dark times to come. And there are prophecies that a Ravenspell will march at her side. I do not ask you this lightly, but please, come to S.W.A.R.M."

Ben looked around fearfully, and Amber could see from his expression just how trapped and miserable he felt.

"When I went to college," Mona said, "I didn't want to go, either. But my mother took me to the campus and showed me around. Once I saw how nice it was, I really wanted to go."

"But the Small Wizards' Academy of Restorative Magic is in a swamp!" Ben said. "You heard Lady Blackpool. It's hot and muggy and full of scorpions. What's the chance that I'll like it there?"

Lady Blackpool smiled slyly. "It is not without its attractions, I think." She looked into Ben's eyes, and her own eyes seemed to be little black stars shining in the night. "Come," she said, "just for a look. You will find that you are honored there. Many will seek your company. Many would like to be your friend."

The offer hung like a cloud of smoke in the air, and Ben's dad said, "Yes, but some will be jealous of your power and will be quick to become your enemies. You'll have to watch your back, son."

Amber could see that Ben was poised on the edge of making a decision. His curiosity about the school, the threat of dangers and the promise of friendship, and perhaps most of all the prophecy that he would have an important part in a future war all seemed to be weighing on him.

"Oh, please come," Amber pleaded. "You won't have to stay if you don't want to, but I would feel so much better with you by my side."

Ben blinked and then bit his lower lip. "All right, but if I don't like it, I'm not staying."

CHAPTER 10

WORDS OF WARNING

A wise man is always eager to listen to good advice. The world is so large, and there is so much to learn, that we must often seek counsel as best we may.
—RUFUS FLYCATCHER

It wasn't until noon that Ben's dad managed to line up a private jet to take the family to Disneyland. The plan was to go there for three days then head to S.W.A.R.M. So many paparazzi were phoning that he couldn't call out. It wasn't until Amber used her own little cell phone to call her friend that they were able to get reservations.

Ben really was looking forward to the trip. He'd spent the entire morning in the spotlights, answering questions about what it was like to get turned into a mouse. He was tired, ready for a break.

The family didn't bring much luggage. They didn't bring any clothes or toiletries. Ben's mom figured that they could buy what they needed in California. So all that they had in their five suitcases was money—five million dollars worth of hundred dollar bills.

There was some discussion as to just who should go on this trip. Amber wanted all of the mice to go, but over the past few days, hundreds of thousands of them had taken up residence in the woods behind Ben's house.

Ben's mom pointed out that this would likely be a very frightening experience for mice, and so she suggested that just a few of the bravest mice should come.

So finally they decided that Ben and Amber would be the only mice to come, along with Amber's advisor, Lady Blackpool. "You'll need someone to protect you," she had warned, "until you've gathered enough mage dust so that your powers return."

The rest of the mice and voles planned to stay in the woods. Ben figured that they wouldn't need anyone to protect them. The mice had their needles to use as weapons if they needed, and, of course, Amber had held a meeting a few days earlier and warned all of the nearby predators that mice were no longer to be a menu item.

Then, of course, the travelers had to decide *how* to travel. "You mice can't just wander around in Disneyland," Ben's mom said. "There are people everywhere, and someone might step on you."

"We'll have to carry them around in a little cage," Butch suggested.

"Not me!" Amber warned, "I've had enough of cages in my lifetime!"

Ben agreed. "We can't go in a cage. We're supposed to get people to *free* the mice."

"It would only be for your own protection," Dad said. "I know . . . how about if Mom carries you in her purse?"

"That would be dark and stuffy," Ben objected.

Amber whispered in Ben's ear, "But I like dark, stuffy places!"

"Not *that* dark and stuffy," Ben said. "Besides, her purse smells like lipstick and chewing gum."

His mom came to the rescue with an idea of her own. "I know: I have that old yellow blouse with the big pockets! The mice can ride in those!"

It was settled. Mom put on her yellow blouse, the mice were loaded into the pockets, and they went to the car. The paparazzi were all over the lawn, flashing pictures and shouting questions.

"Amber," one of them cried, "is it true that you've agreed to do the special effects in the next Harry Potter movie?"

Another shouted, "Who does your hair?" A third asked, "Where do mice go when they go out on dates?"

Amber got confused and tried to answer the questions as fast as she could. "What's a movie?" "Mostly I paw through it myself." "I've never been on a date!"

Dad and Mom had to fight their way to the car, shoving aside photographers, squeezing in as quickly as they could.

Then they were in the car, and everyone sighed in relief. Dad started the engine and began honking the horn, trying to get the paparazzi to move, but they just crowded around, flashing pictures and yelling questions.

Flashbulbs strobed again and again, blinding everyone in the car.

Amber picked up her little red phone and called the president, asking for help.

At that moment, Ben noticed a beautiful little blue butterfly that had flapped in just as the door closed. It flew overhead then landed on the dashboard.

"Hey," the butterfly asked. "Have you guys heard the buzz?" The creature might have been staring at Ben, but he couldn't be sure. It had faceted eyes, and so it could have been looking at everyone in the car at once.

Lady Blackpool nosed up to the dashboard. "Are you talking to me?"

"Of course," the butterfly said.

"What's your name, little one?" Lady Blackpool asked.

"Serena," the butterfly said.

Lady Blackpool smiled wisely. "So, Serena, what's the buzz?"

"The Lord of the Flies has hatched!" she said. "Her name is Belle Z. Bug. She has the most beautiful eyes in the world—as red as rubies—and the most beautiful metallic green carapace. Everyone says that she's the most gorgeous fly, and so friendly and humble. She has this great deal on makeup.

You can get fly-liner just for signing up some friends. And if their friends sign up, then you move up in the plan, higher and higher, and the rewards are . . . well, just impossible to imagine! Just think, you won't have to be ugly anymore. Wouldn't that be great? Want to join?"

Ben's mom shrieked, "Why, that sounds like some vile, twisted multi-level marketing scam to me . . . Sign me up!"

"Yes," Lady Blackpool said more cautiously. "Belle Z. Bug is playing a very dangerous game. She reinforces the feelings of ugliness in her victims on one hand, and then offers them beauty with the other. That is a very great evil indeed."

"You put fly-liner on around your eyes," Serena said. "It makes you look more beautiful. You do want to be beautiful, don't you? Want to join?" The poor butterfly sounded desperate to gain converts.

"I really don't think that *you* need fly-liner," Lady Blackpool said gently. "After all, you're a butterfly and one of the most beautiful that I've ever seen."

Lady Blackpool waved a paw at Serena, and suddenly the little butterfly seemed to waken from a daze.

"What? Where am I?" Serena peered all about in alarm.

"You're among friends," Lady Blackpool said. "You were under a spell cast by an evil fly. She blinded you to truth and reason and to your own innate beauty."

"Oh, goodness!" Serena said in alarm.

"Now," Lady Blackpool demanded, leaning close, "tell me more of what you know. Once this Belle Z. Bug converts the flies to her cause, what does she plan?"

"Oh, dear!" Serena wandered about in a panic. "She's amassing her armies, getting ready to destroy the world!"

"Ah," Lady Blackpool said as if she had expected this news. "And where can I find this Belle Z. Bug?"

Suddenly a black housefly shot up out of the car's grill and shouted at Serena, "Shut your mouth, you filthy traitor! When the Dark Lord rises, you'll be first against the wall!"

Ben's mom warned the housefly, "Quiet! It's not polite to butt in on another person's conversation."

"You can't order me around!" the housefly roared. Then it asked in a confused voice, "Hey, do you *understand* me?"

Ben's mom rolled up a magazine and swatted the fly.

"Ack!" the fly cried. His voice came out rather miserable sounding. "It's not polite," he gasped, "to kill . . ."

The whole family was trapped in the car, surrounded by paparazzi. One of them tried to open the door, but Ben's mom hit the locks. The group had nothing else to do but sit and listen to Serena.

"Go ahead," Lady Blackpool said gently. "Tell us what you have to say."

The butterfly gasped, shocked at the fate of the housefly. "I can't go on," she said miserably. "I'm a traitor to my own species!"

"No, you're not," Ben said. "You're a *butter*fly. You're beautiful and nice—not like some nasty housefly."

"You don't need to convince her to talk," Lady Blackpool told Ben. "There is a spell that compels her to speak." The aging shrew now turned to Serena. "Go ahead, little one, spill your guts."

"The Lord of the Flies has risen at a garbage dump, far to the south of here!" she said. "That's the buzz."

"I see," Lady Blackpool said. "And what are her intentions. How will she attack?"

"I don't know," Serena said. "I only heard that she has come to prepare the world for the Ever Shade—whoever he is—making it ready for his return."

For a long moment, Lady Blackpool considered the news. She glanced at Amber as if wondering what the young mouse might be able to do in the coming battle. But Amber had used up all of her magical energy. She couldn't cast a spell for two more days.

Lady Blackpool sighed. "I will have to face this one alone." Her words hung heavily in the air.

This could be dangerous, Ben knew. He suspected that this Lord of the Flies was powerful—more powerful than any of them knew. Ben asked, "How will you fight her?"

"I have long known that the day would come when I would have to face this monster," Lady

Blackpool said. "I have seen her face in dreams and visions many times. Her power is great, greater than mine. I will have to fight her as best I can, matching my wisdom against her greater strength . . ."

The whole family was sober.

"Is there anything I can do to help?" Ben asked. "Do we need to drop you off someplace?"

The shrew shook her head. "It is no accident that we are flying south. I go now to meet my destiny."

The paparazzi continued to take pictures, lights flashing like lightning. Ben felt trapped, and for some reason, he was unaccountably sad.

A helicopter buzzed over the house and hovered above the car. Black-ops agents fired rubber bullets over the heads of the paparazzi and forced them back, while the props from the helicopter made such a strong headwind that it started to blow photographers' cameras away.

Ben watched the scene from the windows and suddenly had a disturbing thought. "This is what my life will be like from now on," he whispered mournfully. "I'll have photographers chasing me all the time. No matter what happens, even if I turn back into a human, I'll always be the boy who was once a mouse."

CHAPTER II

IN FLIGHT

A single pair of houseflies breeds so quickly that if there were no spiders, bats, and other predators to eat them, over the course of one year the flies' offspring would multiply to the point that they would cover the earth to a depth of half an inch.
—FROM THE RAVENSPELL COOL BESTIARY

Amber had never flown on a plane before, but now Butch had rented a Learjet to take them to Disneyland, a small jet with only a dozen seats. It was very comfortable. Amber had flown in a magically powered flying saucer made from a garbage can lid and a fishbowl. She'd ridden on the backs of mallards and geese. But a Learjet turned out to be the best of all!

The cushions were made from crushed red velvet, and everything was very fancy. There was no stewardess, only a captain to fly the jet, but it did have a nice little minibar filled with root beer, candy bars, and sandwiches.

It took only minutes for Ben's mom and dad to take their seats, and then Amber and Ben raced around, exploring the plane. Lady Blackpool just sat thoughtfully on an armrest while the butterfly Serena landed on the back of a seat and looked out the window.

"If there is anything you need," the captain had said before they departed, "just holler. The intercom here on the plane is voice-activated, and it works both ways."

The captain put on a movie for Amber to watch—*Stuart Little*. Afterward, he went into the cockpit and started the plane. It had gone surging down the runway like a speeding car and had suddenly lifted into the air.

For a moment, Amber watched the earth fall away, the trees and houses growing smaller and smaller until she really couldn't see them at all.

So she watched the movie for a bit. It left Amber confused. It was about a little mouse named Stuart who was somehow living in a human orphanage. Stuart could talk to humans, but didn't seem to have any magic powers at all. Nor did any humans even notice that he was a mouse. He was a very odd mouse who walked funny and wore human clothes. "Mice don't walk like that!" Amber groaned after just a few minutes. "Whoever made this up has never even *seen* a mouse! Why isn't Stuart grooming?"

Ben tried to explain the movie to her, telling her that it was a fantasy. He wanted Amber to relax and just enjoy the film, but she couldn't tell if it was supposed to be serious, funny, strange, or just stupid.

Eventually, Amber got bored. So she merely sat on the armrest while Ben's mom petted her. Mona would gently take her big warm finger and stroke it down Amber's head, from nose to tail, sending shivers of joy down Amber's spine.

I feel so good, Amber thought, *that I think I might just melt into the armchair.*

Amber had never liked a human before—other than Ben, if he still counted as a human—but she was finding that she was growing fond of Mona.

"Tell me how to pet you better," Mona said. "What does a mouse like?"

Amber didn't know for certain, but moments later Mona tenderly rubbed the insides of her ears then pinched Amber's tail and rolled it between her fingers, sending waves of gladness through the young mouse.

Mona leaned close. "I know how you feel about Ben," she whispered.

Amber's heart began to pound. "You do?" She couldn't imagine how Mona could know. Whenever Ben was around, Amber felt as if she might melt from happiness.

"You need to know that I love him, too," Mona said. "He's my son. Even though you might want him to go to your school with you, to S.W.A.R.M., he's still my little boy. I . . . you understand that I can't give him up. I can't just let him go away."

Amber didn't answer. Her heart was breaking.

While Ben scampered around, climbing up the seats and then leaping from the back of one chair to the next, Lady Blackpool only sat gazing ahead as if looking into the future.

Like a faithful watchdog, Serena took up a spot on the chair next to Lady Blackpool.

Finally, Lady Blackpool said softly to Amber, "If anything happens to me in the next few days, I want you to make me a promise . . ."

"Nothing will happen," Amber said hopefully.

"But if it does," Lady Blackpool said, "I want you to promise to go to S.W.A.R.M."

"How will I know the way?" Amber said.

"You'll find the way," Lady Blackpool said. "You have great powers, and even though there are spells that hide the school from the rest of the world, you will find a way."

"Nothing is going to happen to you," Amber affirmed. "Ben and I will protect you."

Lady Blackpool smiled weakly. She whispered, "Life must come to an end. Even for old ones like me. I've seen this beast in a vision, this Belle Z. Bug. I must face her alone. You have no power now—no power to stop her, no power to save me."

"But I can't just let you go alone!" Amber said.

"I let you fight the bat Nightwing alone," Lady Blackpool reminded her. "That was a task you and Ben had to face in order to grow together. Everyone has a time in their life when they must stand alone against evil. Now it is my turn."

"But," Amber said, feeling very sad, "if you know that you're going to lose, why fight at all?"

"I go to my death," Lady Blackpool said, "but that isn't the same as losing. I hope to purchase something with my life."

Serena spoke up and asked, "Purchase something? Like fly-shadow?"

Amber didn't understand. What could her friend hope to gain from fighting a battle that she couldn't win? "What could possibly be worth your life?"

Lady Blackpool said, "I am going to teach you a lesson, Amber. I am going to teach you how to fight a battle calmly, while facing a more powerful foe. I'm going to teach you to use your imagination—not to rely upon force alone. Folks need to know these things."

So they rode through the air, flying over the mist-covered mountains of Oregon, looking at the green fir trees far below, passing through clouds where Amber could practically see the ice crystals hanging in the air.

When the movie was over, Amber closed her eyes for a nap, but she couldn't really sleep. She was too worried for Lady Blackpool.

Suddenly the captain spoke over the intercom. "Be advised that there is a very large, very dark storm cloud ahead. It's kind of a weird one, folks. I don't think I've seen anything quite like it. I'd prefer to avoid any turbulence, so I'll just try to nose around it. If you folks would all put on you seat belts, it would be greatly appreciated."

Ben's mom and dad buckled down, and Amber tried to look out the window to see the cloud ahead, but she couldn't really see anything until the jet suddenly banked hard to the left and dove.

Amber glimpsed the cloud. It wasn't gray but black—as black as if it were formed of millions of bits of rock instead of ice.

But what was weirder was the shape. It wasn't billowy like just any cloud. There was symmetry to it, as if it were showing two sides of something. There were bulbs on top, and a narrow part that might have been a tube, and beneath it was a long tube with a moplike ending.

Suddenly Serena shouted, "Hey, that cloud looks just like a giant housefly!"

Millions of black dots began to move, and the cloud shifted, moving toward them, speeding to intercept them even though their pilot had changed course.

"Those flies can't possibly move as fast as this jet!" Ben said, leaping to Amber's side.

Suddenly there was a grinding noise. The jet shuddered and slowed as if it had been grasped by a giant hand. The engines stuttered to a halt.

In the cockpit, the captain yelped in frustration.

The enormous cloud fly loomed closer, and the moplike ending of its mouth came open.

The cloud lunged, swallowing the jet whole.

Ben's dad started screaming like a girl.

Millions of flies surrounded the jet, swarming onto the plane's frame, grabbing onto the wings. Their droning carried even through the thick glass windows. The plane shuddered and began to alter course, veering south and east.

"They're hijacking the plane!" Ben warned.

"We're being fly-jacked?" Amber asked.

But as soon as Ben spoke, the plane's left wing tilted down then soared back up. The plane began to rock in midair.

"Wait," Ben yelled, "they're trying to tear the wings off!"

Butch slapped himself on the forehead. "Who would have ever thought it—having my wings torn off by a fly?"

"Do something!" Ben's mom screamed.

Ben looked to Amber, and she frowned in frustration. It was too soon for her to use her powers. Still, Amber wondered if she should try.

Lady Blackpool stood calmly upon the armrest of her chair. "Let them take us," she warned Amber. "Don't try to stop them. It requires great power for our enemy to stop this machine, magical energy that Belle Z. Bug will no longer have in battle! Let her waste her powers, and then I will deal with her more easily—face-to-face!"

A fly slammed into the window above Amber and sat for a second.

"Look at that one," Serena shouted joyously. "It's wearing fly-shadow and mask-era and wing wax. Have you ever seen such a beautiful bombardier fly?"

Amber had to admit, the fly did have startlingly bright eyes and a pretty face. But then the wind caught the little bugger and whipped it away.

The jet engines whined and surged back to life. The captain was desperately trying to escape.

The plane groaned forward, trying to break from the grasp of a million flies. There were clouds of them, buzzing all around.

Serena translated the buzzing. "Lady Blackpool, the flies are out to capture you all!"

"Climb higher!" Ben shouted to the pilot. "Flies hate the cold. Try to climb higher!"

Amber wasn't sure if the pilot could hear him, but suddenly the jet throbbed and climbed, angling up. The jet engines sucked in flies by the tens of thousands and then spat out fly-burgers!

"Gross!" Ben's mom said.

Butch covered her eyes with one hand. "Don't look, darling. It will give you nightmares!"

The plane shuddered and trembled. The flies tried to hold on, but the jet was moving too fast. Flies began to peel off the wings in layers, huge rafts of them.

The plane rumbled, nearly free, and soared up into the sky. It raced through a cloud of flies so black that it seemed to be night outside.

"Hooray!" the mice cried.

"What a relief!" Serena shouted.

But Lady Blackpool seemed to be in shock. She stood there gaping. "I don't understand," she said. "This is not what happened in my vision!"

Just as suddenly, the great invisible hand seized the plane again, and the engines roared as the pilot gave them all the juice he had. The plane shuddered. The right engine grumbled, and for a moment the jet seemed to be at the heart of a tug-of-war.

Then the engine burst into flames, exploding in a fireball that singed the wings off a hundred thousand flies in an instant. The flies began dropping in a smoldering rain, and the jet's right wing went with them.

Up in the cockpit, the pilot began to scream. He came running out the cockpit door while pulling on a parachute and cried, "It's every man for himself!"

He wrestled the emergency door open, and there was a rush of air as the cabin depressurized. Then he leapt out of the plane, doing a swan dive through a storm cloud of flies.

Serena was knocked off the plane seat, and the force of the wind plastered her against the breast pocket of Mona's blouse so that she looked like some fancy blue pin.

"Uh," Ben's mom called at the pilot's back, "where are *our* parachutes?"

But it was too late. The pilot had already gone. Flies began whipping through the cabin of the jet, pinging against the wall like hail. The wind was so powerful that Amber feared it would lift her up and send her flying around the room. It might even suck her right out the door. So she just clung to a seat belt with her little paws.

Now would be a good time to have my powers back, she thought. *I was so stupid to have wasted them.*

"Look for the parachutes!" Butch shouted.

The plane bucked and then dropped into a nosedive, screaming through the sky.

Ben's mom and dad looked about frantically, searching through overhead compartments, tossing out water bottles and life preservers.

Flies came bouncing through the cabin, flies in so many colors and varieties that Amber sat astonished. There were the common houseflies and horseflies of course, but there were dozens of strange varieties, too—bee flies that looked like honeybees and pale moth flies with wispy gray hairs covering their entire bodies, even their wings. There were shiny March flies that looked like angry blue-black wasps, and sand flies the color of sand, and fruit flies with brilliant red eyes and metallic green-and-gold bodies, and mayflies that had wings almost like a butterfly and long mandibles for grabbing things. Many were shiny, with strange-colored stripes going across their faceted eyes or bright stripes on their thoraxes.

Suddenly Ben spotted a sign above a small door next to the restroom. He shouted, "Parachutes— over there, Dad!" as he pointed frantically.

Ben's dad raced to the door, pulling hard on the little knob. He banged on it a few times. "It won't open!"

Mona joined him. "It's locked!" Ben's mom cried. "Where's the key?"

As one, both of them looked out the open door, where the pilot had jumped. Mona said, "I think he had it!"

Butch screamed like a girl again then totally went ape. He began kicking the door like a madman.

"Move aside, big fella!" Ben's mom shouted. She gave a mighty kick. The door folded, its hinges turning into twisted pieces of metal. Mona ripped the door open.

On the floor lay the parachutes.

Ben's mom threw hers on, fastening a couple of straps. "Is this on right?" she asked.

"How would I know?" Butch cried, shrugging his own parachute over his shoulder.

The plane seemed to slow, leveling off, and the wind grew less boisterous. Amber suspected that the flies had regained control and were now holding the jet in the air.

Mona raced through the cabin, grabbing Ben and Amber in the high wind, thrusting them into her pockets as fast as possible. Amber dropped into the safety of the big yellow pocket, heart pounding, and found that it was rapidly filling with dead flies.

Serena had joined Amber and Ben and just hid in the pocket, panting from fright, her iridescent blue wings quivering.

One of the flies, its shiny green-and-gold body wounded and broken, peered up at Amber with glistening fly-linered eyes and said in a melancholy voice,

> To-morrow, and to-morrow, and to-morrow,
> Creeps in this petty pace from day to day,
> To the last syllable of recorded time;
> And all our yesterdays have lighted fools
> The way to dusty death. Out, out, brief candle!

Life's but a walking shadow, a poor player,
That struts and frets his hour upon the stage,
And then is heard no more. It is a tale
Told by an idiot, full of sound and fury,
Signifying nothing . . .

The fly's eyes blinked out, and it gasped its last breath.

"Wow," Ben said. "Who knew that flies could wax so eloquent?"

Amber sniffed. "What a wonderful fly. I wish that I had gotten to know him better."

Ben's mom found Lady Blackpool and reached down to grab her. But the shrew raised a tiny paw, warding her back. "Leave me," she said. "It is my destiny!"

"Nonsense," Mona argued. "I don't know where those flies are taking this plane, but I do know that you don't want to go there!"

She grabbed Lady Blackpool, shoved her in a pocket, and before the shrew could object, Mona Ravenspell jumped out of the plane.

Mona went tumbling through the sky, end over end. She'd obviously never jumped from a plane, so she had no idea how to fall.

She was tumbling through a vast, dark cloud of flies, and Amber held on as long as she could. But the wind blew against her at ninety miles per hour, and Amber's little paws couldn't maintain their grip.

She heard Ben shout, "Mom!"

Lady Blackpool shrieked, and Amber saw blurs of fur as both of them got taken by the wind. In no time at all, Amber lost hold and was ripped from Ben's mother.

"Mona!" Amber screamed.

Amber went plummeting through the air. Her body only weighed a couple of ounces, and so for her comparative size, her body gave more wind resistance than a human's body would, so she fell more slowly.

Serena the butterfly was clinging to Amber's tail.

Ben's mom hurtled away quickly down below, disappearing through a haze of flies, while Amber seemed to float.

She screamed and kicked and reached out, trying to grab something. Then she recalled how she'd seen a sugar glider fly at the pet shop. The sugar glider was shaped a lot like a mouse. She'd seen it spread its arms and legs then use baggy folds of skin to soar between tree limbs.

Amber tried the pose, and found that as she spread out, her fall slowed even more. She lifted her nose, arched her back, and splayed out her arms, legs, and tail.

Serena the butterfly shouted, "Don't worry, I can help!" Serena spread out her wings, letting the air catch and lift them.

Amber slowed even further.

She remembered seeing an ant fall from a dizzying height in a tree a few days earlier. Amber had watched it walk away afterward, apparently unharmed.

Maybe I can do that, she thought. *I'm small, and*

my tail has a lot of drag on the air. With Serena holding on, I just might make it.

Amber had often used her tail to sort of hold on to things or to balance on the end of tables when she was getting ready to jump. Now she found that her tail could also act as a tiny parachute.

She floated through the bottom of the cloud of flies and saw the ground far below. She was in California now, a land filled with rocky desert and covered in mesquite and cactuses. Off to the east, an endless blue ocean lay flat and inviting.

Amber only hoped that she would land somewhere soft, like the top of a Joshua tree, or maybe in a nice mountain pool.

Quietly, Amber was riding the wind on her way down when suddenly she saw a little red dot below. The dot rapidly expanded. It was Ben's dad's parachute opening.

A blue dot blossomed next to it and rapidly filled Amber's vision. Mona's parachute had deployed, too, and now Amber was falling straight toward it.

In seconds she landed on it—splat—as if it were a mushy trampoline. Amber sat clinging to it, her tiny claws hooked into the fabric, too frightened to move.

Serena let go of Amber's tail and crawled up next to her face. "Boy, I'm sure glad I have wings right now," the butterfly said. "I'd hate to be you!"

The wind was rushing through Amber's ears, but gradually she became aware of Ben's mother shouting and crying. "Ben? Ben, where are you?"

"Here!" Ben answered. He landed next to Amber atop the parachute with a small thump.

"Ben?" his mother asked.

"I'm up here, Mom!" he shouted.

Mona must have heard him then, because she yelled, "I see you above me! Benjamin Ravenspell, you get down here this instant!"

Ben looked at Amber as if asking for any ideas. He was clinging to the parachute for all he was worth.

Amber considered how to get down. She was terrified, frozen by fear. But through the fabric of the parachute, she dimly spied the ropes that held Mona to the chute.

"Maybe we can climb down!" Amber cried to Ben.

"No!" Ben shouted. "We're safer on top of the parachute. If we're in Mom's pocket when she touches down, she might squash us!"

An instant later, there was a plop nearby. Lady Blackpool pounded down. Amber felt as if it were raining mice.

Amber's little paws were hooked into the parachute fabric right next to Ben's. She looked at him, smiling.

"Whee!" Serena cried. "Is this as fun as the rides at Disneyland?"

Ben just shook his head in wonder.

Moments later, Ben's mom touched down on a brush-covered hill out in the desert. She landed safely, and the parachute just floated to the ground, where the mice scurried off into the grass and Serena flapped about overhead.

Everyone had landed safely, but Butch began to wail in pain or grief.

"Dad, what's wrong?" Ben called.

There was a moment of silence as Butch Ravenspell swiped tears from his eyes, sniffed, and peered down at Ben. "Our money," he said. "We left it all on the plane!" He sank to his knees, wracked by despair.

Amber looked up into the heavens. She could see the flies, a huge cloud of them, carrying the jet off toward the south.

Oh, no, she thought. *I had two million dollars on that plane—enough to buy freedom for millions and millions of mice.*

She wasn't sure how hard it might be to get more money, but she could tell from the expression on Mr. Ravenspell's face that it wasn't easy. She might never get a million dollars again.

Ben's mom studied the flies' movements. Her green eyes took on a deadly gleam—the kind that a person gets just before going into battle.

"They might have our money for now," Mona said. "But I'm going to take it back!"

Amber considered how many mice she might be able to free and shouted, "Me too!"

CHAPTER 12

THE GORGEOUS
GRUB CLUB

*The bad habits and rotten attitudes that we learn from
our parents usually stay with us for life. That is why we
must work so hard to instill them in our young.*
—BELLE Z. BUG

At noon that day, all seemed right with the world
to Belle Z. Bug. Her minions were scattered across
the dump before her; flies covered the land as far as
the eye could see, a black mass of seething bodies.

Belle reached up and stroked her magic charm
bracelet, making sure that it still touched her skin.
Youth gave her beauty, and beauty made her per-
suasive. So long as the charm bracelet remained
touching her skin, she felt secure.

"I'd like to introduce a new program," Belle
shouted to the flies, "a special new plan designed
just for our darling little maggots. It's called the
Gorgeous Grub Club, and it's open to every maggot more than an hour old . . ."

A strange droning filled the air, a sound louder than the buzz of flies. Belle stopped her speech and watched over a line of trees to the north, seeing something large buzzing toward them.

At first she thought it was a giant fly like her, and Belle's hearts skipped a beat.

She had not realized how lonely she felt, being a monster and the only one of her kind. Sure, she had fly-shadow and mask-era to make her beautiful, the most gorgeous fly on earth. She had her lipstick on, and she had set the hair on her back with a stylish new perm.

But who was it all for? Without a male fly to impress, all of her beauty was wasted. Its only purpose was to rouse the envy of other flies.

But in the next instant, she saw that it wasn't a fly. It was a small, yellow airplane. It came buzzing toward the dump, and Belle Z. Bug got a sick feeling in the bottom of her abdomen.

Belle had been expecting a plane. Her vast magical powers had let her see that Amber was flying on a silver jet. But this wasn't the plane that she had been waiting for.

"Uh-oh," a nearby green bottle fly said, "this can't be good!"

With ten thousand eyes, it isn't hard to look about. Belle could see every direction at once, except for a little blind spot in her rear. In a glance, Belle realized that a strange silence had fallen over the landfill. The huge dump trucks that had been lining up all morning had stopped coming.

"It's an attack!" Belle screamed in warning. "Everyone, take to the skies. Pull that plane's wings off!"

The plane roared toward them. Just as the enormous mass of flies leapt into the air, a cloud of noxious gray gas suddenly poured from the back of the plane.

Two miles away, at the edge of L.A.'s enormous landfill, flies that had taken to the air met the cloud and immediately began to plummet, dropping like flies.

Death is coming, Belle realized. *Death is coming for us all.*

Her flies were helpless against a well-armed crop duster.

But Belle had her magic and a fierce will.

She smiled up at the plane.

So, she thought, *the humans want to make a fight of it! That's admirable of them. And a fight they shall have!*

She felt deep down inside herself for the source of her power. She was weak. She'd cast several spells only moments before in her struggle to capture Amber's plane. She felt drained, but Belle had power still.

She only needed a little.

She cast a spell, a slight wish. With a thought, the poison tanks on the crop duster exploded inward, releasing their noxious gases into the cockpit. The fumes filled the interior of the plane, fogging the windows.

Seconds later, the pilot kicked open the door

and leapt out, clutching at his throat and coughing.

He was so close to the ground that his parachute didn't have time to open. Instead, he hit the ground with a heavy thud.

A mass of Belle's minions roared into the sky to take vengeance on the man.

Meanwhile, some of the fumes from the crop duster had begun drifting close.

Belle felt the vile chemicals clogging the pores of her skin. She twitched, a fly's equivalent of a cough, and tried to breathe. It was a struggle. The poison irritated her sorely, made her ten thousand eyes burn. But she would live through it.

Belle ground her mandibles in outrage. *Humans—the worthless scum!*

She raised her voice so that it carried across her innumerable throng. "Okay, folks," she said with a cheery smile, "new program, starting now! I'm going to give each of you a little magic power.

"When you buzz into a human's ears and whisper my name, Belle Z. Bug, you'll have the power to make them do something naughty! I want each of you to go out now and start taking a little vengeance! Any fly that gets fifty human converts by sundown will get our newest shade of hot pink carapace color!"

Amid shrieks of delight, the flies lifted into the air in a vast and indomitable cloud.

* * *

Governor Harold Shortzenbeggar was the greatest man alive. The fact that he won the Mr. Galaxy Pageant was proof that no man on earth was his equal physically.

But his greatness did not end there. Not only was he the strongest and best-looking man of his time, but he had also spent his time studying and had become the most fabulous actor ever.

Even being a governor wasn't hard for him. He found that people wanted to be led as much as grasshoppers wanted to be herded, but he was up to the challenge.

Governor Shortzenbeggar took the task to heart, and after only a few weeks, he'd quickly become the most dedicated and efficient leader the world had ever known.

Only in legend could men be found that rivaled Governor Shortzenbeggar—men with names like Hercules, Atlas, and Attila the Hun.

Now, he stood outside the L.A. landfill with a pair of high-powered binoculars, peering at the rising cloud of flies. He'd seen the death of the fearless pilot that had led the air-strike against the dump.

He shook his head in dismay. "I hate to see men dropping like flies," Harold said to the crowd of worried dump truck drivers at his back. "It should be *flies* dropping like flies!" he explained in his thick Swiss accent.

The danger here was very apparent. California has a fly problem. In a state where so much fruit is grown, a number of exotic fly species have taken hold. Sometimes, when the weather is right, it leads to vast fly hatchings. Normally these are just various fruit flies that hatch—particularly white flies, which eat tomatoes, strawberries, and other vegetables.

The governors of California have tried to keep this quiet for generations. After all, if people realized that the state has such a nasty fly problem, the tourists might stop coming.

So the state kept a small squadron of crop duster planes working at all times, spraying the vineyards and orange groves.

The War of the Flies was a constant one, a battle that mankind could not afford to lose.

Governor Shortzenbeggar didn't like to keep secrets from his loyal supporters. He would have preferred to be honest. The fly problem wasn't such a bad thing. It wasn't like the things that were constantly going on off the coast of Florida, with the great white sharks gobbling down tourists like popcorn, and giant squids sinking boats, and the pirates, and . . . well, all that other stuff.

Harold couldn't see how Florida's governor could sleep at night, what with his secrets.

Still, from time to time, a special group of flies hatched. It was called a "bloom" of flies.

This time, a mutant fly led the swarm—a real nasty one—most likely with telepathic powers. The governor had been forced to battle monsters like it before.

Fighting it would take more than a man. It would take a superman.

Resolutely, the governor turned and began to stalk away. He couldn't allow his dump truck drivers to go back into the hot zone, not so long as the monster fly was a threat.

One truck driver shouted at his back, "Hey, where are you going? You can't just leave these flies in control!"

The governor came to a halt. Without turning, he said to the crowd, "I'll be back!"

CHAPTER 13

THE UNLUCKIEST CHAPTER EVER

When building hotels, the builders will often skip
building the thirteenth floor, going from floor number twelve
straight to floor number fourteen. The reason for that is a concern
that the thirteenth floor will be unlucky. I decided to
skip this chapter for the same reason.

I was going to tell you how the flies began to take
over the world. I was going to tell you how they buzzed
into downtown Los Angeles and whispered into people's ears to do
naughty things. Like, for example, when moms parked at grocery
stores, they began to take up two parking stalls, while
complete strangers began pointing at one another just for
fun. Barbers gave Mohawks to businessmen. People in
restaurants began eating with their mouths open and
then wiping their greasy hands on the tablecloths.

But then I realized that if I told you all of the nasty things
that happened, there might be tenderhearted children reading
this, and they'd get bad dreams. So I'm not going to tell you.
Just use your imagination. If there was anything
bad that could happen, it did!

—THE AUTHOR, DAVID FARLAND

CHAPTER 14

LOST IN THE WILDERNESS

*It is not wise
To listen to flies*
—COB

Fortunately, Ben Ravenspell's dad had stashed a few thousand dollars in his pockets as "folding money."

"We can use it to hire a taxi," he said when he broke free from his parachute.

The only problem was that they had bailed from the airplane out in the wilderness somewhere in a desert full of mesquite bushes taller than Ben's dad's head and yucca plants with broad spikes for leaves.

The small group gazed down from the hilltop where they'd landed.

"If we only had a cell phone," Butch said. But Amber's little cell phone was lost.

"What do we do?" Ben asked. He felt weak and very vulnerable here in the desert. It was only April, so it wasn't very hot. In fact, it was rather pleasant. But Ben couldn't see any sign of a lake or stream for miles. He worried he might die of thirst.

"Maybe we should just wait here for help," Ben's mom suggested. "I'll bet that our pilot sent some sort of distress call."

"That bozo?" Butch asked. "I don't think so. I didn't hear him calling for help."

Ben knew his dad was right. The pilot had access to a two-way speaker system in the cockpit. They'd been able to hear everything he said, and he hadn't called for help.

"Boy, what lousy luck I'm having," Butch said. He squatted on the ground, head drooping.

"Cheer up, hon," Mona said. "Look at the bright side: we made four million dollars this morning!"

"Yeah, but we lost it all before noon," Butch said. "And I think we're all going to die!"

"Perhaps we should start walking," Lady Blackpool suggested. "I have found that one cannot go too far without running into a human road of some sort. Besides, it will be good for Ben and Amber. They need to collect mage dust. I suppose I'll need it, too."

"Okay," Ben's mom said. She picked up the mice and shrew and stuck them in the big pockets of her blouse. "I think we should go west from here. When we were falling, I thought I saw a freeway in that direction. I'm sure that I saw some orange groves."

"West it is, then," Butch said, glancing up at the sky. The sun was almost directly overhead. "Uh, which way do you think is west?"

"This way," Mona said, pointing to a path through the brush.

"Are you sure you want to carry us?" Ben asked. "I don't want to weigh you down." As soon as he spoke, he realized how dumb he must sound. Altogether, two mice and a shrew couldn't weigh more than four ounces.

"I think I can manage," Mona said.

Ben and Amber were thrust into one pocket, and Lady Blackpool had gone into the other. Serena the butterfly chose to fly on her own, dipping from flower to flower as she traveled.

"Wow, your mom sure is great!" Amber whispered to Ben as they walked. "I mean, she's *carrying* us."

"Yeah," Ben said, and he felt kind of weird inside. A couple of weeks ago, he hadn't realized how cool his mom could be. He'd seen her dirty house and her lazy habits. But now here she was, marching through the wilderness, leading them toward the lair of an evil fly, and she had a strange look in her eyes—a cold intensity that Ben had never seen before.

"Mom, you're different," Ben said. "What happened to you?"

He looked up. From his vantage point, he couldn't see much more than the inside of his mom's nose.

Her voice came out sounding kind of sad. "Two weeks ago, when I woke up and you were gone, I realized that I could have been a better mother, Ben. So I decided to try to be the kind of mom that I knew I should have been."

Ben thought for a moment and then admitted, "I think you're a great mom."

That brought a soft smile to her face.

For long hours they marched through the desert, over rough rocks and through tall brush. There were lots of cactuses among the mesquite—little barrel cactuses with bright red flowers and prickly pears with their strange leaf buds.

There was lots of life here in the desert, more than Ben would have imagined—meadowlarks and sparrows leaping about in the brush, and other kinds of birds, too, like scarlet-chested wrens. Ben saw a cottontail rabbit disappear into a thicket under a cactus. The desert was quiet and beautiful.

Ben would never have admitted it, but he decided that he liked being on another adventure. He liked being out in the wild with Amber.

But this was even more fun, because now he had his mom and dad with him. He felt safe with them.

Amber sat next to him, and she pointed out a little mouse hole in the grass, just beneath a cactus. A pair of fine red rocks rose up to either side of it.

"What do you think lives there?" Amber wondered aloud. "A mouse or a vole?"

"In the desert," Ben said, "I've heard that there are lots of kangaroo mice. They can jump like me."

"Wouldn't it be fun to meet them?" Amber asked.

Ben had to admit that it would.

"If you could have a burrow anywhere in the world," Amber asked, "where would it be?"

That was a big question. Ben hadn't thought much about it. The world was such a big place. "I guess in Hawaii," Ben suggested. "They say that it's real pretty there."

Ben's mom and dad had passed the little burrow now, so Amber said, "I think I'd live back there—with a cactus for my roof, and nice big rocks on each side of my burrow. You would never have to worry about cats or coyotes trying to dig out your burrow."

Ben had to admit that it did look like a nice little burrow, but he wondered if Amber was hinting at something. He knew that she had a crush on him, and she wanted him to stay a mouse. But sometimes he worried that she wanted him to be her boyfriend. Was she hinting that she wanted to live in that little hole in the ground with him?

"That cactus might keep out the coyotes," he admitted, "but you'd still have to worry about rattlesnakes."

That made Amber fall silent, and she gave him a nervous glance.

As the day wore on, Ben's mom began to tire. Her breathing deepened, and so much sweat soaked through her blouse that Ben felt as if he were in a sauna instead of her pocket. They'd been gone for hours and hadn't found any water.

Suddenly, Butch pulled the money out of his pants pocket and tossed it on the ground.

"What are you doing?" Mona asked. She stooped to pick up the money. "Are you so tired that you don't feel like you can carry a few extra hundred-dollar bills?"

"I'm littering," Butch said. "I like to litter. Uh, I mean, at least I've always *wanted* to do it!"

Ben's mom gave him a curious look and then shoved the money into her own pocket. "Maybe we should rest," she said. "I think that the sun is getting to you."

A fly buzzed overhead, circled Mona once, and buzzed off.

Butch turned to walk away, but Mona jumped forward and stepped on the heel of his shoe, so that it came off. "Ha!" she cried in glee. "Gotcha!"

Ben had never seen his mother play such a childish prank before. Yet he suddenly had his own strange compulsion.

If I were at school right now, I'd run down the hall! he thought. He imagined how free he would feel, running as fast as he could then stopping and sliding over the polished floor. Nothing in the world sounded as fun as running down the halls.

Butch turned and glared at Mona as if he might hit her for taking off his shoe. He crouched for an instant, trying to get his shoe back on, and he scowled up at her.

"Don't you dare lunge at me!" Mona shouted. "I . . . I . . . I've wanted to tell you this for years:

your mom is such a turkey that when she comes for Thanksgiving next year, I'm gonna baste *her*!"

A wild fierceness blazed in Butch's eyes. They gleamed with insanity. Suddenly Ben noticed a fly buzzing around his dad's head, and Butch leapt forward. He grabbed the money from Mona's pocket and held the bills up. Then he savagely tore them into little pieces, right in front of Mona's eyes.

"Litter!" he shouted gleefully, throwing the shredded bills into the air. "Litter, litter, litter! I'm a litterer!" The scraps of hundred-dollar bills floated down like confetti.

"What in the world are you doing?" Mona shrieked. "That's all the cash we have!"

"Don't worry," Butch said. "I'll just rob a pizza parlor and get some more! Or . . . or maybe I'll make Ben write a book. Or maybe I'll sell these stupid mice into slavery! How much do you think we could get for a magic mouse?"

Butch leered, the crazed expression on his face deepening. Mona lunged forward, startling him so that he tried to leap away. But she stepped on the heel of his left shoe again, pulling it off.

Butch growled like a wounded bear and whirled, trying to escape from Mona. She latched onto the back of his shirt, and the two of them became locked in a dance, Butch trying to get away while Ben's mom tried to stomp on the heel of his right shoe.

"Let's get out of here!" Amber screamed, and she leapt from Mona's pocket.

Ben and Lady Blackpool did the same, and Ben thumped to the ground. He took shelter beneath a cactus and sat trembling while his mom and dad circled each other.

Butch stuck his tongue out at Mona and waggled it like a dog. He rolled his eyes back in his head so that they turned white then used his fingers to flare his nostrils out. He made grunting noises like a pig.

"Hogs! Hogs! You're all a bunch of hogs!" he shouted. "And I'm not going to do anything you say!"

Ben's mom gave a bloodcurdling scream and leapt in the air, and then karate-kicked Butch right in the gut.

"You crazy creep!" Butch screamed, doubled over in pain. He bent over to pick up a handful of sand and throw it in her face, but just as he scooped it up, Ben's mom shoved him into a patch of cactus.

Butch yelped in outrage. "I'm gonna . . . I'm gonna poke you in the eye!"

He leapt up and grabbed Mona. He tried to poke her in the eye, but she dropped her head a little and bit his finger.

Butch screamed as Mona kicked him in the shins. He fell, pulling her down on top of him into a pile of cactus. They were both yelling and growling. Ben had never seen such a great fight in his life!

"Stop!" Serena screamed. The blue butterfly dipped in from above and fluttered between the two grown-ups. "Stop fighting! Don't you see what's happening? It's the flies. The flies are telling you to do this!"

Immediately Ben glanced up and saw that, indeed, a pair of flies circled above his parents.

Now they buzzed toward Serena and grabbed her by the wings. Serena shrieked and tried to escape.

The flies shouted, "Traitor, we'll show you!" as they caught her from behind. The flies grabbed her back and clung on for a second.

Serena struggled to climb back into the air, but the evil flies snapped her wings off. Serena dropped, her wings fluttering to the ground like leaves.

The two evil flies laughed maniacally and leapt into the air.

It happened so fast that Ben was helpless to stop it.

His mom and dad began circling each other, ready to brawl.

Ben still wanted to run in the halls at school, but now an even deeper compulsion struck. Next time he went to the school, he was going to chew gum in class then leave a big, juicy wad under the teacher's desk!

Ben glanced up; the flies were circling overhead, just above him.

"Cover your ears!" Lady Blackpool shouted. "Everyone cover your ears! The flies are putting some kind of curse on you all!"

"Your ears, Mom—cover your ears!" Ben shouted.

He put his little paws over his own ears, drowning out the sound of the flies somewhat, and almost immediately the strange compulsions began to fade.

Lady Blackpool stood beneath the blade of cactus and raised a paw in the air. She muttered an incantation.

Birds that dart, birds that glide
Come and eat these evil flies!

Instantly, birds came careening through the mesquite brush, shooting between the branches like arrows.

They weren't fancy birds—just little brown sparrowlike creatures, some with a bit of red or yellow on their chests. But did they fly fast!

They raced into the glade and darted around Ben's mom and dad almost like hummingbirds, stopping and flapping motionless in the air, then plunging off in some new directions. In seconds, they had each gobbled down a couple flies.

The buzzing ceased, and Ben took his paws off of his ears.

But the birds remained. In a few seconds, more of them appeared, and then more, landing in mesquite bushes, perching on the spines of a large cactus. Dozens of them fluttered near, then hundreds.

Ben's mom and dad stopped fighting. They both crouched warily, eyeing one another for a long moment, as if afraid that the other would attack.

Mona's face softened, and she fought back a tear.

"Oh, cuddle-pumpkin," Butch said. "I love you. I'm so sorry."

"And I love you, my kissy-lips," Mona replied.

Suddenly the two lunged at the same time. But instead of fighting, they just stood hugging.

While Ben's parents traded apologies and kisses, Ben looked about. Birds kept coming. A great flock had begun to gather from across the desert.

"What's going on?" Amber asked. "What kind of birds are these?"

"They're called flycatchers," Lady Blackpool said. "Most of them. Others are bee-eaters. They're excellent fliers, and all of them eat flies."

"But . . ." Amber said, "there are so many birds. Where are they coming from?"

"They're scattered throughout this desert," Lady Blackpool said. "They're plain enough in color that you don't notice them until you are looking for them. But we will need their help. We'll need an army of them if we are to confront Belle Z. Bug!"

Lady Blackpool gave Amber a sidelong gaze and added, "Remember, Amber—never waste your powers by fighting if you don't have to. You can often enlist the aid of others."

Amber looked solemn as she considered the lesson.

As the flycatchers gathered, a mournful young Serena came crawling up to Ben. "Oh," she lamented, "my wings, my beautiful wings!"

Ben's heart nearly broke. He reached down and picked up the wounded butterfly, holding her under his arms as if she were a wiener dog. He stroked the fine blue-gray hairs on her antennas. "Don't worry," he said. "I'm sure that we can find a vet who can sew those wings back on."

"Just—just carry me to a flower patch and leave me," the butterfly said mournfully. "I can crawl from flower to flower. It will be a joyless existence, but I suppose that it will be my lot from now on."

"Nonsense," Lady Blackpool said. "You're our friend, and we'll care for you."

Lady Blackpool and Amber hopped off through the grass and cactuses; they returned moments later, each gingerly carrying one of Serena's wings.

CHAPTER 15

OUT OF THE DESERT

*Good things come to those who wait. Better things
come to those who go out and get them.*
—LADY BLACKPOOL

Amber scurried through the wilderness, weaving
her way past cactuses, plunging through the grass,
leaping over stones. The brush grew so thick here
that she couldn't see a hundred yards in any direction. Butch led the way, with Mona right behind.

Amber just hoped that they had a better view
than she did of where the group was heading.

Ben and Amber had decided to walk for a
while, in the hopes that they would be able to
gather more mage dust closer to the ground.

As the group made their way through the
desert, a great flock of birds swarmed around
them, flitting from tree to tree. It felt spooky having them so near. Time and again, Amber would

feel a bird's shadow flit overhead, and each time she cringed a little and found herself freezing in place.

Mice have an inherent fear of hawks, especially when a bird's shadow passes over them.

Amber grew very nervous and miserable indeed.

Yet she was grateful to have the bee-eaters and flycatchers darting about, snapping up every housefly and horsefly in sight.

The wicked insects had given the group no more trouble. Considering the size of the vast flock of birds, Amber wasn't surprised.

But the birds made poor Serena even more nervous than they did Amber.

The wingless butterfly just hid in Mona's pocket, muttering over and over again, "I don't want to be eaten! I don't want to be eaten!" At last Serena settled down at the very bottom of the pocket and said, "I think I'll just hide in here until this whole darned war is over!"

Twice that afternoon, the group heard helicopters buzzing nearby, but the mesquite grew so tall that even though Ben's mom and dad waved, the helicopters didn't stop.

"They're searching for us, I think," Butch said. "They must know by now that our plane went down. Our flight plan called for us to be in Los Angeles hours ago."

"Maybe," Ben's mom said hopefully. "But how will they know where to look if they can't find any wreckage? Our plane got carried off by those flies."

And who knows where they took it, Amber thought.

For long hours they walked, until Amber felt parched from lack of water. The sun began to slant toward the horizon, and the sky took on a reddish glow.

Ben seemed fretful, worried.

At last they stopped for a rest, and Ben sat beneath the shade of a yucca bush and preened, using his paws to comb through his whiskers, and then he brushed the hair around his face. Amber used her teeth to dig a burr from the fur on her belly.

Ben told Amber what was on his mind. "I'm glad we have these birds to protect us," he said. "But can you imagine what must be happening in the cities right now? You saw how my mom and dad started fighting, and they're in love. What must be going on around the rest of the world? People have no protection from this plague of evil that the flies have brought."

Amber couldn't really imagine what might be happening. Back in the pet shop, she'd known an evil mouse that used to bite her tail. She tried to envision humans biting each other but couldn't quite picture it.

"It makes me wonder," Ben said thoughtfully, "what will happen when the Ever Shade comes . . ."

Amber peered at him, and she wondered too. If Belle Z. Bug was just one of the Ever Shade's minions, what would the others do? And what would their master be like?

Lady Blackpool had been sitting nearby, and now she crept closer. "This war that has begun," she told Ben, "isn't like the little skirmishes you fought with that bat and worm. The Ever Shade will not be satisfied until the entire world is under his control—including mankind."

Ben grew sober at the thought. "You said that the Ever Shade came a long time ago," Ben told her. "But the world has changed. We have guns and bombs—"

"And they will avail you nothing," Lady Blackpool said. "You saw how effective bombs were against Amber's magic just yesterday. The Ever Shade will wrest mankind's weapons away from them, and use them against the humans."

Ben had no answer to that, and the thought of a magical creature taking control of human technology truly frightened Amber.

I have to keep Ben, Amber told herself. *I'll have to make him my pet human. It's not just for me—it's for both of us. It's for the good of the whole world.*

Yet Amber had to wonder. *Is that the kind of mouse that I am—the kind who would steal the freedom of a friend?*

She didn't want to be that kind of mouse. She didn't want to hold Ben captive. She wanted Ben to stay with her willingly.

But she thought of the flies and got an idea.

Maybe I could pretend that they buzzed in my ear, she considered. *I could take Ben captive just as long as I needed and pretend that the flies made me do it.*

It wouldn't really be wrong, she told herself. *I wouldn't be keeping him for selfish reasons. The world needs him. In fact, I wouldn't really be keeping him at all—just borrowing him.*

"Ben," Amber said, hoping to bring the subject up gracefully. "I don't think any of us can imagine how much evil these flies are doing. If what happened with your mom and dad gives us any clue, then things must be bad indeed." She waited a moment for Ben to nod his agreement and then pressed on. "If one little fly is giving us so much trouble, I wonder what will happen with the Ever Shade. I wonder . . . how I'll fight him without you."

Ben gave her a sharp look, and Amber's heart began to pound from fear. He knew what she was leading up to.

"You're turning me back into a human," Ben told her. "You promised!"

But Amber suddenly recalled a promise that Ben had once made to her. "And you promised to help free the mice of the world first, didn't you?"

Ben's eyes flashed in outrage. "I did what you asked. I helped you free the pet shop mice. That's all that you were asking for—when you *forced* me to make that promise!"

"Yet you promised," Amber said, "and that is all that counts!"

Lady Blackpool asked, "What? Are you trying to back out on a bargain?" Outrage and alarm sounded in the shrew's voice.

"If I did," Amber said, "it wouldn't be for me—but for all of us. The world needs Ben, just as it needs me! The world needs him to be my familiar!"

"You cannot *force* Ben to remain with you," Lady Blackpool said. "That would be a great evil that would canker your soul. In time you would rot from the inside—from the heart.

"To force another into service is a violation of the good wizard's code," Lady Blackpool warned. "The masters of S.W.A.R.M. would never give you entrance to their school if you brought Ben as your slave—if you made him your puppet! The very fact that you are entertaining the notion makes me wonder if I have been wrong about you. This casts matters into a whole different light!"

"But Ben promised to help me," Amber said.

"A promise made under the force of a threat is no promise at all. Ben must choose his own path in life. You must give him his freedom."

"After he tried to feed me to a lizard?" Amber demanded. Ben wasn't entirely faultless, either.

Lady Blackpool backed away from Amber a bit, as if she thought that the mouse was dangerous. "Amber, if your magical powers are to be used for good, then they must come from a heart that is pure. We cannot use our powers to blackmail others, or to take away their freedom to make their own choices. 'Magic cannot be properly controlled or handled by use of force'—that is the great creed of S.W.A.R.M. 'Instead, if our powers are to be used for good, we must always cast our spells out of compassion—with a heart that is full of gentleness and meekness and love unfeigned.'"

"Uh," Amber began to say, but words failed her. She couldn't think of a good argument against the shrew, at least none that Lady Blackpool was likely to entertain. She sounded certain of her course. There was a warning in Lady Blackpool's voice—a tone of regret and dismissal.

"There can be no other way," Lady Blackpool said. "If you cling to your evil ways, your heart will darken. You will grow to be like the Ever Shade, and in the end you will either join forces with him and walk in his shadow, or you will become as corrupt as he is—and ultimately challenge him for power."

Amber thought that Lady Blackpool was crazy. That could never happen to Amber. She shook her head. "I'm not like that!"

"Not yet, perhaps," Lady Blackpool said. "Let us hope that you never become like that." She turned away, and Amber stood for a moment, feeling ashamed.

Yet I have to keep Ben, she told herself. *I can't afford to set him free . . .*

* * *

It was two hours from sundown when Ben's parents finally found a road. It was a little blacktop lane, winding among some low hills.

The group had hardly set foot on it when they heard police sirens in the distance—lots of them, coming through the desert toward them, just beyond a hill. The group sat waiting expectantly for the police cars to come. They waited and waited. But the police were coming awfully slowly.

After what seemed like forever, a big-rig truck thundered over the hill. Its tires were all flat. It was riding on its rims, shooting a cloud of sparks in the air. Thirteen police cars were chasing it at maybe ten miles per hour, their sirens wailing and their lights flashing.

The parade of vehicles crawled toward the little group.

"Hey," Butch said, "I've seen chases like this on television! They happen all of the time in California. I wonder who's driving? Maybe it's O.J.!"

The police cars kept creeping along. One tried to swerve and accelerate past the truck, but the big rig veered right into it, sending it flying into the ditch. An angry police officer leapt out of the ruined car and fired a shotgun into the back of the truck, opening a gaping hole in the cargo container. Potatoes came bouncing out of the hole.

It was all very thrilling to Amber.

The truck eventually crawled close. Its air horn blew, trumpeting like a charging elephant, and Amber looked into the cab. An enormous red toad drove the truck, grinning like a madman!

The truck drew close and then swerved to hit the group. Everyone leapt across the ditch just as the truck approached, spitting up gravel and hurling hot sparks into the grass.

The evil toad cackled and shouted, "Beware

the Toad Warrior!" Then the truck rolled past, and all of the police cars kept chasing it hardly faster than a mouse could run.

The sparks from the truck had set off a tiny fire in the grass, and Butch was still stomping it out when a helicopter came careening over the ridge, heading straight toward them. It hovered overhead while the flocks of flycatchers and bee-eaters scattered from the propellers like leaves fluttering before the front of a storm.

The helicopter touched down, and a couple of cheerful-looking CIA agents jumped out. "Mr. and Mrs. Ravenspell," one of them said with a phony smile, "I'm glad to see that you're well. I strongly advise that you come with us for your own safety!"

"Come with you where?" Ben's mom asked.

"We'll brief you in the chopper," he replied, opening his lapel just enough to show his gun in its shoulder holster. Then he stepped aside so that Ben's mom and dad could pass.

Lady Blackpool halted, refusing to go with the men. "It is not my destiny to hide in safety. I have seen it in a vision. I must go to a place called the Los Angeles Landfill," the shrew insisted. "Can you take me there?"

The CIA agents looked at her as if they were unsure whether they should be negotiating with a shrew. "We can't take you folks there," one said. "They've got big trouble brewing there."

"I know," Lady Blackpool said. "That's why I've gathered an army." She nodded toward the huge flock of birds.

An agent studied her and smiled dismissively. "We don't need the help of a flock of sparrows. The United States of America is not going to let itself be manhandled by a bunch of flies!"

"Magic flies . . ." Lady Blackpool corrected. "And only a fool would underestimate the power of their evil."

"We're not underestimating them," an agent replied. "We know what they're capable of. The whole state of California has fallen under their sway. We have hooligans drag racing down the streets through hospital zones and pedestrians jay-walking everywhere. We've got fat people wearing skimpy bathing suits on the beach. It's horrible!"

"But we also have our own secret weapon," the other agent confirmed. "We've got Governor Shortzenbeggar!"

"You go and have your governor fight them," Lady Blackpool said dismissively. "I have a better plan!"

Ben's father and mother looked torn. They wanted to go on the helicopter, but they didn't want to leave Lady Blackpool behind.

"I don't understand," Butch said to the CIA agents. "Why is it that *you* two can resist the flies?"

One of the CIA agents reached up and pulled a black plug out of his ear. "IPods," the agent said. "Just turn up any Souza march, and you can't hear anything else."

That comforted Amber. At least the CIA seemed to know what they were doing.

"Come on folks," one of the men said. "Time's a wasting. We're only fifty miles from the landfill. I can drop you off in a safe zone a few miles out. But that's as close as we'll go."

Amber looked to Lady Blackpool; the shrew stood firm. She seemed intent on making her own way. "Come with us," Amber begged. "They have secret weapons."

"So does our enemy," Lady Blackpool said. "I'll make my own way, thank you. But you can go with them if you wish. The choice is yours . . ."

Ben followed his parents and hopped into the helicopter. Amber didn't like the idea of hiking through the desert any farther, but she suspected that Lady Blackpool wouldn't be walking for long. It wouldn't take much to cast a spell and call some large bird to give her a ride. Now that the humans were leaving, the shrew would be able to travel faster alone.

Hurriedly, Amber raced to the helicopter and jumped in just as the doors closed.

She leapt up on the dashboard and looked out through the tinted bubble of the cockpit to watch Lady Blackpool. Even before the helicopter lifted from the ground, a red-tailed hawk came sweeping out of the sky. It swooped low to the ground, and Lady Blackpool leapt onto its back without the hawk even stopping. Soon Lady Blackpool was borne away, her army of birds flitting along behind as silently as ghosts.

CHAPTER 16

MUTAGENIC MIRACLES

All that is required for good to triumph over
evil is for evil flies to do nothing!
—BELLE Z. BUG

The sun was dropping rapidly at the landfill, descending into a haze of red that lined the western hills. The day was nearing its end.

Belle Z. Bug watched it with her ten thousand eyes, and her heart felt heavy. Trouble was brewing, she knew. The humans had stopped bringing their tribute of garbage again. That meant that an attack was imminent.

Somehow the knowledge buoyed her spirits and gave her a little thrill.

But what the humans might try next Belle couldn't quite guess.

The humans were at a disadvantage. Her flies were everywhere, descending upon the streets of

Los Angeles. The news crews were catching it all, sending it over dozens of television channels. Belle could see the images in her mind.

People had begun looting in the merchant districts, and fires roared out of control all across the countryside. She saw images of police officers playing chicken with each other on the freeways.

"Kill the flies!" the reporters were warning on some channels. "The flies are making us do it!"

But other reporters were laughing maniacally and yelling into the cameras, "Save the flies. Flies are our friends!"

Amid such chaos, Belle didn't see how the humans could put together any kind of organized response to her takeover. Even now, her flies were sweeping across the country, through every state and region. Within the hour, she anticipated that the entire continent of North America would be groveling at her feet.

Well, let them grovel, she thought.

She put a smile on her face and turned to address her adoring fans. Trillions of flies had gathered, and their buzzing filled the air, as constant as the beating of her hearts.

"Are you feeling tired?" she called to them. "Do you need a little lift to get airborne? Then you should try one of my latest products . . ." She waved toward a nearby container of waste from a nuclear reactor. "I call it Atomic Sludge Fudge. One gulp in the morning and you'll have endless energy all day! There's no power like *nuclear* power!"

The flies cheered the news and buzzed approvingly. Belle strode along the prow of her little boat, raising her arms to encourage the cheers.

Now was the moment that she had been waiting for all day. She had been having her research and development team working with various toxic chemicals, mixing them in containers of discarded hair gel. Now she had developed a formula that was just what she needed to keep the humans off balance in the coming battle.

"And for our latest development," she said, "I've got a special treat for our double platinum members! Today only you're invited to come forward and get a dose of Mutagenic Miracle Grow, made from only the finest-quality mutagens. One dose and you'll get *big* results!"

A tiny whitefly stepped forward, beaming proudly. It had the full treatment of Belle's products—from the fly-liner to carapace color. He was indeed a truly beautiful little whitefly, with sparkling eyes and a perfect complexion.

Belle Z. Bug strode forward with an eyedropper and squeezed out a single droplet of gray-green ooze. It splattered on the fly, and for a moment the tiny thing looked as if it would drown.

Suddenly it began to grow, and grow, and grow—until soon he was a strapping monster of a fly, all glistening white and larger than a hound.

There were gasps of excitement among the crowd. "Look," someone shouted, "an abominable snow fly!"

"Now," Belle said gleefully, "if a single drop can do this for a little whitefly, imagine what it can do for a horsefly. Imagine what it could do . . . for *you!*"

The flies began to cheer wildly, and they surged forward to get a dose of Mutagenic Miracle Grow.

Belle smiled secretively. Now if the humans attacked, they'd find a foe worthy of battle.

CHAPTER 17

THE TROJAN GARBAGE TRUCK

*It is only when we are faced by the most troubling times
that we discover who our true friends are!*
— LADY BLACKPOOL

Governor Harold Shortzenbeggar slung a rocket launcher over his back, shoved a pair of miniature machine guns into his boots, and hefted his .55 machine gun.

All around him, CIA sharpshooters stood with cans of fly spray poised, squirting any fly that dared get too close. The governor was making his final preparations for his assault on the state's largest landfill. The smell of fly spray filled the air in a toxic cloud, much like the odor of a Los Angeles freeway.

His iPod was blaring into his ears one of his favorite songs from the band Throat Kultcher:

I am the Trashman,
And I'm takin' you out tonight!
I'm wagin' war against human garbage,
And my guns are blazing bright!

He punched the FORWARD button on his iPod and instantly brought up the familiar strains of Queen's "Another One Bites the Dust."

He smiled in satisfaction. It was the perfect music to launch an assault with.

"The first rule of battle," he explained to one of the CIA agents, "is that you should always go into it with the proper inspirational music!"

The governor was standing beside an enormous dump truck. Technicians in the back were setting the timer on the Big Bug Bomb. The governor took some comfort in the knowledge that even if he didn't make it out of the battle alive, the bomb would detonate, and the casualties among the flies would be devastating.

Once the technicians were done, they grabbed some shovels and covered the bomb with garbage, a tempting mix of horse manure and an assortment of foods one would find at a picnic—potato salad, watermelon, black olives, and the greasiest fried chicken west of the Rockies.

The agents heaped the truck high with garbage and then topped the entire mess off with a maraschino cherry.

The governor was just getting ready to hop into the truck when he spotted a helicopter drawing near.

He waited for it to land and watched as the Ravenspell family leapt out.

"Good to see you," Governor Shortzenbeggar said to the family. "I'm just getting ready for our assault on the landfill. Care to join me?"

"Uh, no thanks," Butch Ravenspell said, nervously eyeing the rocket launcher and various machine guns.

"Oh, come on," the governor begged. "They're just flies. I could really use your help." He smiled down at Amber and Ben, who had poked their heads out of Mona's pocket.

"I'm sorry," Amber apologized, "but I'm afraid that I won't be able to come. I've used up all of my magic and can't cast a spell yet for two more days."

"Oh, what a shame," the governor said. "Well, I guess I'll just have to have all the fun blowing them up." He tossed a grenade launcher on the seat inside the truck and then started to climb in.

"Are you sure all of that is really necessary?" Butch Ravenspell asked. "I mean, why not just wait for a cold spell so that the flies die off?"

"This is a magical fly," Amber said. "She'll find some way to protect herself, making her live longer."

"Yeah," Governor Shortzenbeggar said. "Besides, Los Angeles doesn't have cold spells. Lucky for me, I've got guns."

He turned the key in the ignition and began pumping his foot to give the truck some gas.

"Wait a minute," Amber shouted. "Maybe . . . I guess maybe I should come."

"You can't!" Ben objected. "You could *die* if you cast a spell."

There was a hissing noise as a couple of CIA agents zapped some infiltrators with fly spray.

"Well, it's been a whole day since I cast a spell," Amber said. "I'm thinking maybe I could just cast a really tiny spell—and only if I have to."

Ben shot back, "We should ask Lady Blackpool."

"Who's she?" Governor Shortzenbeggar said.

"She's a friend," Amber explained. "She's a shrew with magic powers—and she's coming with an army of birds that can eat the flies. Maybe Ben's right; maybe we should wait for her!"

The governor bent his head in thought. "Hmmm . . . a green solution to the problem. I kind of like the idea. On the other hand, the longer we wait, the more things will go wrong. Right now there is rioting in the streets. I'm afraid that if we wait even for five minutes, the whole state could go down the toilet."

Amber gave him a long look, and her little ears seemed to droop. "Okay," she said. "I guess I'll come with you!"

"Yay!" the governor said. "We are going to have such fun!"

He scooped up Amber and Ben in his hand and set them on the dashboard of the truck so that they could see.

"Wait a minute!" Mona Ravenspell shouted. "You're not going without me!"

"Okay," the governor said, "what kind of

weapon would you like: automatic shotgun, or maybe a bazooka?"

"Just give me a flyswatter," Mona said. "I've lived in a dump all my life, and I can swing a fly-swatter like a ninja master!"

A CIA agent handed her a pair of flyswatters, one for each hand.

Mona jumped into the front seat and asked, "What's the plan?"

The governor glanced down, trying to figure out how to work the gears on the truck. "You ever hear of the Trojan horse? Back in ancient times, the Achaeans were trying to take over the city of Troy. They couldn't break down the walls, so they built a big, hollow horse out of wood, and shoved it up to the city gates, pretending it was a gift. When night came, some warriors hidden inside the horse crept out and opened the city gates, let-ting in an army.

"My plan is something like that . . . except that I'm using a garbage truck instead of a horse. And instead of warriors, I'm going to sneak in a bomb."

The governor slammed and locked his door, started up the truck, honked the horn twice so that everyone would get out of his way, then floored the gas and went roaring off into battle.

"I'm sorry that I don't have iPods for every-one," he said. So he cranked the truck's radio up to full power. He found a classical station, one that was playing Wagner's "Ride of the Valkyries."

The road ahead was four lanes wide; it wound through some hills where the dead vegetation had turned brown. The governor shoved the gears up a notch and hit eighty miles per hour. He wanted plenty of speed, just in case the flies had set up a roadblock.

The sky overhead was red, and the sun slanted in from the west. The whole sky looked as if it glowed from distant fires. In another hour it would be dark.

He knew that he was getting close to the dump when the flies appeared. They began smashing against the windshield like a grisly rain. The skies overhead suddenly grew dark as a cloud of flies rose from the dump.

Harold Shortzenbeggar blew the horn on his big rig. "Come to Papa!" he shouted in greeting.

He grabbed the truck's radio and called in. "This is Little Bo Peep, over."

"We read you loud and clear, Little Bo Peep," a voice shot back over the radio.

"I'm at the gates of the wasteland. A cloud of sheep is rising above it, but I have not sighted the Lost Sheep. Hold your fire until you get my signal."

"Roger. We're locked and loaded and awaiting your signal . . ."

Mona Ravenspell frowned. "What's going on here?" she asked. "I thought we were going in alone?"

"Oh, we are," the governor answered. "But I've got the air force on standby with a few missiles, just in case we need them . . ."

The cloud of flies was growing thicker. The ugly insects filled the sky like a plague of locusts, blackening the heavens. It was so dark that it felt as if thunder and lightning should fill the skies.

But the only sound was the ominous humming of flies, a sonorous buzz that seemed to come from everywhere and nowhere at the same time.

Flies were bouncing off the windshield like hail, making a sound like popcorn popping in a pan.

The truck's automatic headlights flipped on, but so many flies covered the lights that they were almost useless.

A few flies made it up through the air vent, into the cabin of the truck. Mona Ravenspell made quick work of them with her flyswatter, and Ben Ravenspell leapt out and stabbed a huge horsefly with the little needle that he used as a spear. It sat on the needle like some grotesque shish kebab.

"Way to go!" the governor congratulated Ben.

Suddenly Governor Shortzenbeggar gave a cry of horror. Amid the black cloud of flies, something enormous came hurtling toward him—several somethings. He squinted, but could not see them clearly. Too many flies clouded the way.

Then he saw it: a squadron of enormous flies sped toward him, giant flies as big as cows!

"Holy moly!" the governor shouted. He grabbed his radio. "I've got bogeys coming in at twelve o'clock, about a dozen of them!"

"Bogeys?" the voice on the radio asked.

"Superflies!" the governor screamed. "They're as big as buffalo some of them! As big as wild boars. I could use a little help here!"

"The packages are on the way," the voice assured them.

The superflies buzzed the truck, seven of them winging to the left, six of them zipping to the right. They sped over and around the truck in a blur, moving so fast that it gave the governor a cramp in the neck just trying to look at them.

One fly yelled in an amplified voice, "That's far enough. Stop the truck and surrender your cargo!"

Oh, great, the governor thought. *Just what I need—talking giant flies!*

The governor gritted his teeth. "Let's party!" he said, reaching down into his boots and silently pulling a machine gun out of each one.

He hit the brakes, and the truck ground to a halt. Immediately a cloud of flies descended. He peered into the rearview mirror and saw the giant flies land. They began buzzing loudly, giving orders to the lesser flies. These monster flies moved with incredible speed.

He'd seen flies dart about on hot days, moving almost quicker than thought. Well, these flies were doing the same, only they were giants.

Hordes of little worker flies landed on the garbage and began picking up the greasy chicken and watermelon then lugging it through the air. Sometimes thousands of little houseflies clung onto a piece of chicken at once. They worked quickly. Too quickly. In only seconds the superflies had uncovered the bomb.

"Hey, what's this!" a giant fly demanded. It reached down and tried to pick up the bomb, but it was too heavy and far too large. The bomb, short and squat, filled the entire bed of the truck.

"It's a trap!" a second fly shouted.

Now was the perfect time to attack.

"You want something to eat?" the governor shouted at the flies. "Try some bullets!"

He whipped out his machine guns and slammed the barrels through the back window. A hail of bullets swept through the bed of the truck, but the superflies were fast—too fast. The governor had tried swatting flies on hot days, and as a child had been amazed at how they could dart off so quickly that they could seem to disappear.

That's what happened when he opened fire. A dozen of them had been hanging on to the side of the truck, but instantly they leapt into the air and seemed to vanish!

Only two lowly flies took lead in the rain of bullets.

Mona Ravenspell sat there with her flyswatters for a moment, looking at the useless things. "Forget this!" she said, tossing them aside. She grabbed a rocket launcher, pointed it toward the front windshield, and sat fiddling with some buttons and levers.

"Hey," the governor told her, "I wouldn't push those if I were—"

Slam! A giant superfly hit the windshield, shattering it into ten thousand pieces. The monster fly hovered menacingly over the hood, glaring into the cab of the truck with its faceted eyes. The fly had a metallic-green body with a golden sheen to its back. A wide reddish brown band, like the mask of a raccoon, ran across its black eyes. The governor couldn't help but think that it was a rather handsome fly.

"Looks like we're going to have a little picnic after all," the superfly said. "And you're the main course!"

In that instant, Mona Ravenspell accidentally set off the rocket launcher. A rocket blasted out, catching the superfly in the midsection.

"Mother!" it whimpered. The fly hurtled backward, out over the hood, and suddenly exploded in a million pieces.

Tens of thousands of angry flies began to pour through the cab. Ben Ravenspell leapt onto the dashboard with his needle and valiantly began to skewer them like an expert swordsman.

The governor saw a blur in the darkness and realized that the superflies were coming back. He whipped out his machine guns and laid down cover fire, clearing the area above the hood. He was hoping to keep them at bay.

Suddenly he heard the wrenching of metal and looked out the driver's window of the truck. A giant fly had landed, and it was using all six legs to peel the metal door from its frame.

The governor wheeled, tried to get off a shot, but instantly the fly vanished. The governor glimpsed it flying off—carrying the door with it!

A giant fly hit the back window, and the governor tried to wrench around. He glimpsed another one of the monsters out the front.

"They're everywhere!" Mona Ravenspell shouted.

"Not for long!" the governor assured her. He began firing both machine guns at once—one through the front window, one out the back.

That's when he heard the buzz. Something grabbed him through the open door hole, something enormous. A fly ripped the guns from his hands with two arms then tried to yank him from his seat.

Fortunately, he was buckled in.

He grappled with the giant fly, biting it on one of its hairy arms. Mona Ravenspell screamed. The governor glanced down at Amber and tried to yell, "Do something!" But his mouth was full of fly leg.

The monster grabbed him with all six arms and buzzed angrily as it jerked him again. If the governor had been a normal man, the power of the beast would have broken every bone in his body. Fortunately, for one of his movies Governor Shortzenbeggar had been fitted with a skeleton that was made from a titanium alloy.

His bones did not break, but the seat belt snapped.

The fly ripped him from the cab of the dump truck and carried him high into the air.

"Aaaaagh!" the governor wailed. "I'm a gonner!"

CHAPTER 18

SUPERFLIES

*When the odds are overwhelming, the wise man retreats,
neither in haste nor fear, but calmly and with all of the resolute
fierceness of a warrior marching into combat.*
—TSUN TZU

As Benjamin Ravenspell lunged, skewering a fly, he whirled and saw the governor's legs lifting into the air.

Ben's mom dropped the missile launcher, looking for another weapon. All that she had were the fly-swatters. "I'm gonna need a bigger swatter!" she cried.

Trillions of flies blackened the sky; Ben knew they couldn't fight them all. "Do something!" he shouted to Amber.

A huge shadow appeared just outside the passenger window. A bluebottle fly as big as a hippo roared in anger and ripped the passenger door from the car. Ben's mom screamed in terror and grabbed for a fallen machine gun.

The fly lunged quicker than a blink and snatched Ben's mom from the truck.

"Help!" she cried as the enormous fly lifted her into the air.

"Do something!" Ben shouted to Amber. More giant flies buzzed into view, surrounding the truck. They hovered in the air, peering through every smashed window, glaring into the cab. "Amber?"

"I did something!" Amber said. "Let's get out of here!"

Ben froze in fear. He'd imagined that the only reason that one of the giant flies hadn't eaten him was because he was sitting still or because he was so small. Now he realized that there was some kind of spell protecting him.

"What did you do?" he asked.

"I made us invisible—" Amber said, "at least to flies. I just sort of wished that . . . they wouldn't notice us!"

It was a small spell, Ben realized.

One superfly shouted, "Hey, everybody! Stop buzzing! I think I hear something in there."

As one, the giant flies all landed, and little flies dropped too, covering the truck. The sound of buzzing faded to a distant hum. The flies looked into the truck, their enormous multifaceted eyes searching every corner. One big fly stuck out his mop and began licking the hood of the truck, as if tasting it, trying to get their scent.

The only sound was the blaring of the radio.

Ben's heart pounded as the giant flies investigated the truck. He was afraid that they might have super-hearing and might hear his heart beating.

He was even more afraid for his mother. The giant flies had taken her, and he didn't know where. It was up to him to save her. They'd taken the governor, too, but Ben didn't care about that so much, even though he did like the movies the governor had starred in.

"I hear something," a giant sand fly whispered. "There's something in there. Something small . . ."

"It's just the radio," a buffalo-sized horsefly said.

A vast whitefly climbed into the back window. "I hear it, too!"

Ben stopped breathing, wishing that his heart would stop beating. Suddenly he heard a whining sound up above, and a pair of cruise missiles came shooting overhead. They landed a hundred yards away and sent off a pair of small fireballs casting a red glare. The explosion lifted the truck off the ground and left it rocking.

But it wasn't the explosion that did the damage. Instead, a huge green gas cloud erupted where the missile had landed.

"Flee!" shouted a fly, and the superflies roared into the air, wings pounding, seeking to escape.

Dead and dying flies began to drop onto the truck, pinging down like volcanic ash. All around, Ben could hear the dying flies whimpering and bemoaning their fate.

Thank heaven for pesticides, Ben thought. *From now on, I'm always going to keep a bottle of Raid handy.*

More cruise missiles whined overhead, twenty or thirty of them, and began exploding in a wide spread. Ben suddenly remembered the huge bomb in the back of the truck. "We'd better get out of here," he shouted to Amber, "before our bomb blows!"

Amber leapt out the door on the passenger's side. Ben followed. It was a long drop, but his fall was cushioned by dead flies.

He looked down at the hundreds of varieties—the beautiful green-and-gold body of a long-legged fly, the frightening yellow-and-black stripes on a hoverfly, the humped back of a robber fly. There were so many colors and types, he was in awe, and many of them were surprisingly beautiful. He wasn't sure if it was because they were wearing make-up or if he had just never noticed how pretty flies could be before.

Amber took a few hops. She picked up her front paws and stared at them in disgust. "I'm never going to want to groom again!" she said.

Ben felt the same. "Where to?" he asked.

"I think they took your mom that way!" Amber said, pointing off toward his left. "But if you want, we could just sneak out of here. That would be the safest thing to do."

She gave him an odd sidelong look. Her brown eyes were glazed from weariness.

Does she really think that I'd leave my mom? he wondered. *Of course not.*

Yet he knew that Amber felt like he was abandoning her, and he wondered if the mouse was testing him, trying to see how true he could be.

"We can't just sneak off and do nothing," Ben reasoned. "We have to rescue my mom and Governor Shortzenbeggar."

"Well, all right," Amber said wearily. She sounded sick, as if she might faint. But she turned and led the way.

So the pair of mice raced along the road, deeper into enemy territory. The skies were a pitch black. It seemed that no matter how many flies were killed, more took their place.

* * *

Amber felt done in. Casting just one little spell had cost her dearly. She felt the wizard wearies coming on strong. Her tail felt as heavy as if it were made of lead, and her stomach was churning—sure signs that she'd overdone it.

She didn't want to disappoint Ben, but she knew that she couldn't cast another spell today. To do so might kill her.

She wondered if she could do that—cast a spell while knowing that she would sacrifice her life by doing so.

I could do it for Ben if I had to, she told herself. *That would show him! Maybe he's the kind who could leave me in a pinch, but he'll see that I'm not that kind of person.*

She didn't want to go deeper into fly territory. She felt so sick and terrified that she could barely keep from fainting.

Yet she managed to put one paw in front of the other, time after time, to keep on going.

An enormous explosion suddenly lifted Amber into the air, and the force of the blast tossed her forward. She glanced back behind her and saw an enormous fireball roaring up into the sky where the truck had been. A toxic cloud was shooting up like a mushroom, dark green in color. Amber gazed into the cloud and for an instant saw the image of a grinning skull. The Big Bug Bomb had exploded.

Ben raced up beside Amber. "Cover your nose!" he cried. "It's not safe to breathe that stuff."

So the two huddled together side by side, closed their eyes, and waited for the gas cloud to disperse.

"Oh, my gosh," flies began to cry all around. "They're using Diazinon! It's the end of the world!"

The flies buzzed in anger and fear, and it seemed that the heavens were falling as millions and millions plummeted from the sky.

Is it too much to hope, Amber wondered, *that one of these gas bombs or missiles killed Belle Z. Bug?*

Yes, it did seem like too much to hope. Belle Z. Bug was a wizard, and a powerful one. It was going to take more than a little poison to get rid of her.

Amber opened her eyes just a bit. Dead flies littered the ground to a depth of a good six inches, and they were still raining down. Amber and Ben had to scurry in order to keep from getting buried. In some places, huge drifts of dead flies were building like snow in a blizzard.

But there was one sign of hope. The darkness in the skies had lessened, and now Amber could see the falling sun on the horizon, like a huge bloody eye.

CHAPTER 19

MANKIND'S LAST HOPE

*A cousin of mine once fell into a pail of milk
with some friends. His friends swam about for a time
but soon gave up and let themselves drown.*

*My cousin, however, kept kicking and fighting until after a few
hours the cream on top of the pail began to turn to butter, and he
was able to sit on it, regain his strength, and finally hop out.*

*From him I learned this lesson: never cease to struggle.
Though your hope may be depleted and even desperation can
no longer sway you, never cease to struggle.*
—RUFUS FLYCATCHER

Governor Harold Shortzenbeggar struggled valiantly as the superfly bore him over the junkyard. He grabbed one of his captor's arms and broke it, then bashed its eye with his fist, breaking a dozen facets. It felt like bashing his hand through some weird cardboard box coated with rubber.

"Hah," the fly said, mocking his efforts. "I can still see you, loser!"

The fly socked the governor in the eye for good measure, and for a moment all that the governor could see were stars.

He heard cruise missiles whining below, and there were dozens of concussions as they dropped their payloads. Noxious gas rose up in clouds, but the giant superfly weaved between them, avoiding the danger zones.

"Oh, what a bad day I'm having!" the governor mourned.

It wasn't easy to be a governor, but someone had to do it.

Why not me? he told himself. *Why not the best man on earth?*

Yet today, he wished that he had just stuck to making movies. Being a movie star was so much easier.

No, he remembered. *No it wasn't. There were those idiot directors making me repeat my lines over and over again, and those greedy movie studios always trying to steal my money, and the fans always begging for autographs.*

I'd rather be here any day, fighting giant flies! Yes, this is the good life!

The fly had reached the top of the landfill and came in low, like a helicopter gunship cruising above a jungle.

Suddenly Governor Shortzenbeggar saw the enemy camp beneath him. There was a large boat down there—a small discarded yacht with a broken hull. It seemed to be sailing over a sea of junk. And on the deck he could see a knot of giant flies in a circle.

One large fly was speaking to the crowd.

That must be their leader, he thought. *They're taking me to their leader.*

He pretended to faint, giving it his best Oscar-worthy performance. He let his eyes roll back in his head; his whole body slackened.

He still had one trick up his sleeve—or actually, tied to his belt. It was a hand grenade.

He thought, *If I can just get close, maybe I can lob it under their leader.*

But he knew that his plan was dangerous. These flies were superhuman fast. If he tossed a grenade, they'd just leap into the air and buzz away.

I have to come up with a better plan, he thought. Then an idea struck him. *Oh, I know! I won't* throw *the grenade. I'll just pull the pin and blow myself up along with the enemy!*

It was a huge sacrifice, he knew, but sometimes a job required you to do a little extra.

Behind him, an enormous explosion ripped through the sky; a fireball lit up as the Big Bug Bomb went off. Beneath the glare from its giant green mushroom cloud, the giant flies stood for a moment in shock, gazing at the approaching death cloud.

The governor's captor buzzed down to the group and hurled Harold Shortzenbeggar to the ground. "Grovel, human!" he commanded. "The almighty Belle Z. Bug demands respect."

A huge fly strode forward, looking gorgeous in her mascara, eye shadow, lipstick, and various other forms of makeup. Her carapace was painted hot pink, but he could see that it wasn't her natural color.

"So," she said, glancing toward the spreading mushroom cloud, "I suppose that we have *you* to thank for all of this mayhem?"

"You're going to thank me?" the governor said. "That's a relief! I thought you would be mad!"

Belle Z. Bug chuckled dangerously. "One human—one measly human—killed millions of my followers."

"Billions, maybe," Harold Shortzenbeggar said, "if I'm lucky." Very sneakily, he put his hands on his hips and pulled the pin on his grenade.

In forty seconds, he thought, *we're all going to get blown to smithereens.*

An enormous fly buzzed in and tossed Mona Ravenspell onto the deck of the boat beside him.

"I stand corrected," Belle Z. Bug said. "*Two* of you caused all of this trouble!"

"Leave her out of it," the governor said. "She's an innocent bystander. I always like to have a pretty girl at my side when I go roaring into combat."

He stood for a moment, clenching the grenade in his fist.

"Is that right?" the fly asked Mona.

"I just came for my money," she explained. "It was on the plane your flies stole!"

Belle spat. "Money? I don't care too much for money. Money can't buy me love."

Well, the governor thought, *I've got about twenty seconds now before we all die in a grisly explosion. But I have to wonder: is it fair for me to kill Mona Ravenspell, too?*

I mean, on the plus side, I would be killing the world's most powerful and evil fly. But on the minus side, I'd be killing an innocent woman.

How would that look in the newspapers tomorrow? What if the paparazzi get photos? It would certainly mar my reputation.

I think I'm about down to five seconds now, and then this whole hilltop will be riddled with shrapnel . . .

Governor Shortzenbeggar hurled the grenade in a lightning-fast pitch, popping Belle Z. Bug right between the eyes. He screamed and threw himself on top of Mona Ravenspell, just to make sure she didn't get hit by any shrapnel.

The monster fly groaned in pain, staggered a step, and then passed out on the ground. All of the superflies gasped in shock or roared in outrage. They stared at the live grenade. "Wow," one of them said, "he just conked our boss on the head. I'm completely baffled! I mean, how does one respond to such an outrage!"

The governor looked at the grenade and thought, *You're nowhere near as blown away as you're going to be!*

Mona Ravenspell struggled, trying to get out from under the governor. "Get off me, you brazen womanizer. I'm happily married!"

The governor counted in his mind: *One; two; three . . . three and a half; three and three quarters; uh, foooooooouuuuuur?*

There was no explosion.

Belle Z. Bug climbed up to her feet and groaned.

"A dud?" Governor Shortzenbeggar asked. "My last grenade, the only hope for the human race, and it was a dud? Probably made in China!"

Belle Z. Bug picked up the grenade and tossed it as far as she could. It bounced down into the garbage pile like a rock and just sat there.

The mushroom cloud from the Big Bug Bomb was beginning to settle, and the poison gas had finally begun to reach them. Belle Z. Bug stuck her mop in the air and blew.

Suddenly a strong wind gusted, blowing all of the poison away, back to the north.

Belle Z. Bug glared at Harold Shortzenbeggar. "Didn't your mother ever tell you never to mess with a sorceress?!"

"She might have," Governor Shortzenbeggar said as he climbed to his feet and dusted himself off, "at the same time that she told me the rule about always eating my broccoli. Of course, I never followed that rule, either."

The monster fly huffed and if possible, it seemed that her green-and-hot-pink exoskeleton darkened with rage. Her antennas did a little angry dance as she tried to think of some torment worthy of his crimes. "You," she said. "You tried to kill me! You tried to kill my people!"

"You can't blame a guy for trying," the governor said.

"You will pay for your audacity!" Belle roared.

Now the governor knew he was really in trouble. He thrust out his chest and demanded, "So what you going to do about it?"

Belle Z. Bug cackled insanely. "You think you're so great—the perfect specimen of humanity. Well, I'm going to do to you what someone should have done a long, long time ago!"

"What, erect a statue?" Harold Shortzenbeggar asked.

"Hardly," Belle Z. Bug said as her ruby eyes seemed to boil with inner fire.

CHAPTER 20

BEN TO MOM'S
RESCUE

*Often all that is needed to accomplish the impossible is for
one humble creature to come up with a well-made plan.*
—RUFUS FLYCATCHER

Beneath the glowering sunset, Ben and Amber
raced over the waste, guided only by the sound of
Governor Shortzenbeggar's screams.

He wailed and hollered, begging for death, but
the evil flies carried on their gruesome torment.

Ben and Amber climbed through the rubbish
piles, scooting under broken couches, tiptoeing
along a bit of water pipe, balancing on paint cans,
holding their noses when they passed the smelly
places.

Everything was covered by the corpses of slain
flies in a hundred varieties.

At last they found the governor. He wasn't hard
to see. Belle Z. Bug had her henchmen holding him

at the very peak of the rubbish pile. Ben's mom was nearby, and a pair of giant flies held her, too!

"Keep him still!" Belle Z. Bug shouted. "Keep him still." But the governor thrashed and fought like a madman. But it was no use. The superflies clung to him like death. "Now pour it on!"

Though the flies tortured him, Ben couldn't see any marks on him, no gaping wounds or blood. In fact, Ben couldn't see that the flies were hurting him at all.

Then it happened. One giant mantis fly held up an eyedropper and let some liquid fall.

There, at the side of the governor's neck, something horrible began to grow, like a grotesque, black jack-o-lantern. Ben could see eyes popping out on it, but the mouth was strange and twisted, and all too soon it began to sprout odd protuberances—antennas and a mop.

It was the head of a giant fly!

"Careful," Belle Z. Bug told the others. "Don't get any of the Mutagenic Miracle Grow on him—just on the limbs we're grafting on."

"Please, no more!" Governor Shortzenbeggar cried.

The newly grown head pivoted and looked him in the face. "Please, no more!" it mocked. Then it looked to Belle Z. Bug and said, "Will somebody do me a favor here and lop this extra head off?"

The flies all chortled.

"It worked!" Belle Z. Bug called. "We got him to grow an extra head. Now let's try a new abdomen!"

"I want to grow another head on him," one of the flies argued. A third shouted, "Let's give him a wing!"

Amber stood in shock, horrified. "What are they doing?"

Ben watched for a second just to be sure. One giant fly reached up and snatched a tiny fly out of the air, then tenderly twisted off one of its appendages.

"They're sticking fly parts on him," Ben realized, "and then making them grow. They're going to turn him into a giant fly! I saw that on a movie once. I hate it when that happens."

Harold Shortzenbeggar peered at the spot where the flies had dripped the Mutagenic Miracle Grow, and now he began to scream as a third arm—a long hairy fly arm—began to sprout from his ribs.

The fly's head whined, "Seriously, this guy is screaming right into my antenna! Can someone please remove this . . . obnoxious tumor?"

"Hey, buddy," Harold Shortzenbeggar said. "This was my body first. If anyone is going to get his head lopped off, it's you—even if I have to do it myself!"

"Oh, yeah," the fly head said, "what are you whining about? You know the old saying, 'Two heads are better than one'? Well they are! I'm smarter than you, and I'm nowhere near as ugly as you!"

Amber crouched low and whispered, "What can we do to help the governor?"

Ben thought hard but couldn't come up with any good plans. He considered stealing the eye-dropper, but that wouldn't help much. He also thought about attacking the giant flies, but that didn't seem wise.

He only had one weapon—his spear.

"It doesn't matter if the rest of those giant flies live," he told Amber. "But someone has to kill Belle Z. Bug, and I guess that someone should be me."

He brandished his needle and wiped off the gore from the flies he'd killed earlier.

"What are you going to do?" Amber asked, her voice a fearful little squeak.

"I'm going to jump up in the air and bury my spear right between that monster's eyes!" Ben said.

"I'm afraid," Amber cried. "Don't leave me."

"I have to," Ben said. "They've got my mom . . ."

Amber fought back some tears. "You really are the most courageous mouse I've ever known, Ben Ravenspell," she said. She lunged forward and hugged him.

Ben turned and began scrambling up to the top of the heap, wading through a drift of dead flies. It was like trying to wade through snow; he fought his way forward a few feet and then looked back. He'd left a little trail among the dead flies.

I'm invisible to the flies, he reminded himself, *but they still might see my footprints*.

Amber crept along behind him. He didn't know if she planned to help or if she just wanted to watch, but she had begun following in his path.

"No!" Governor Shortzenbeggar cried. "Not the wing! Don't put a wing on me!"

Ben peered ahead as the poor tortured victim renewed his struggles to escape. At least his screams provided a diversion for the monsters.

"Hold still!" Belle Z. Bug shouted. "Or you'll end up with a wing growing out of your nose!"

The torture resumed, and Ben decided to make his move. He leapt uphill in mighty bounds.

The flies were all hunched over, looking at the governor, but they had so many eyes that it was impossible to tell where they might be looking. He only hoped that the governor's distractions would keep them from noticing the little trail of mouseprints that appeared among the dead flies.

Suddenly the governor lunged like a wild man and kicked a superfly in the pancreas. The other flies buzzed angrily and fought to control the governor.

Ben leapt up and grabbed the gunwale of the discarded yacht. There weren't so many dead flies on the floor there. Ben raced closer to the victim and stopped just outside the circle of giant flies.

Belle Z. Bug was straight ahead, pacing nervously, enjoying the show as one of her enormous flies poured a drop of Mutagenic Miracle Grow onto a wing.

It began to sprout from the governor's back, a huge, nasty thing that looked like it was made from wax paper. The governor had struggled so much that the flies had set it in the wrong place—instead of growing from the governor's shoulder, the wing sprouted from his kidney.

"Wow," a big fruit fly said, "that looks great! Let's give him another one!"

But Belle Z. Bug had a better idea. "No, hold him down while I pull the wing off. *Then* we'll grow another one!"

All of the flies laughed hysterically, and the big fruit fly jumped on the governor and held him. Belle Z. Bug crawled forward to do the evil deed.

Ben heard a little scuffling noise behind him. It was Amber. She'd crept up to him. "Now," she whispered in his ear. "Do it now!"

Ben gripped his needle spear and studied the monster's head. He was pretty sure where its brain was—right between those enormous faceted eyes. The light was still good, though the sun was dipping between the low hills.

Ben cautiously hopped over the deck of the ship, sneaking between two huge superflies posted as guards, and drew near Belle Z. Bug.

The giant fly had painted her body hot pink, and with her makeup on, Ben had to admit that she was truly beautiful—all except for a child's charm bracelet around her neck. It was a silly thing, with little plastic tennis shoes and four-leaf clovers and whatnot. It didn't go with the outfit at all.

I wonder why she wears that? Ben thought.

He was just about to leap and plunge his spear between her eyes when his mother screamed, "Ben, Amber, run for your lives!"

Ben looked up. His mother was being held by two giant flies. She stared right at him.

Oh, no! he realized. *I'm invisible to the flies but not to my mom!*

Belle Z. Bug whirled and glared at Ben.

"Assassins!" she shouted. Ben's cover was blown, so he took a mighty leap, aiming his spear right between her eyes.

She lifted her mop the way an elephant lifts its trunk, and she blew . . .

A powerful wind hit Ben like a hurricane, catching him midleap. The force hurled him backward and up into the air. He went somersaulting crazily, like a tumbleweed in a hurricane.

The same wind lifted Amber up, and both of them went flying.

"Have a nice trip!" Belle Z. Bug shouted. She began to cackle.

Ben and Amber went hurtling high into the air, tumbling and spinning until Ben felt sick to his stomach.

Just like a ride at Disneyland, Ben thought as the wind carried them high over some trees and sent them hurtling miles and miles away.

CHAPTER 21

LADY BLACKPOOL

I do not fear death. I look forward to it with hope and anticipation, for I know that death is just a new beginning.
—LADY BLACKPOOL

The wind carried Amber and Ben for perhaps fifteen miles, until finally it gave out and they began to tumble. They dropped into some deep marsh grass that cushioned their fall then fell into a shallow pond.

Wet, sick to her stomach, and miserable, Amber slogged from the water into the shallows. Darkness was falling. All around frogs croaked. Mosquitoes hung thick in the air.

Ben climbed onto the grass behind her and whispered, "We've got to get out of here. There are bullfrogs in this pond, all around us!"

"So?" Amber said.

"They can eat a mouse!" Ben said. "I saw one do it on the Discovery Channel."

"Oh, great," Amber groused. "Isn't there any place that a mouse can go to just get away from it all?"

The two of them hopped up into the tall marsh grass and crept through a jungle of cotton-tails. The mud around the base of the plants had been pounded flat, so that they could sneak along quietly. Only once did they catch sight of a frog— a big, blue-eyed devil off in the cane.

They raced away, and it didn't give chase.

Soon the pond fell behind, and they reached the edge of an orange grove. Ben stopped at the grass line and looked up, scanning for hawks or owls.

"Hop, stop, and look!" he warned.

"Where are we going?" Amber asked.

"Back to the dump," Ben said.

"But there's nothing we can do there. Belle Z. Bug has broken my spell. She can see us now, and I don't have the power to cast another."

"My mom's there," Ben said. "I have to help her. I can't just stay here and do nothing."

"You can stay here with me," Amber said. "We could hide out in a field and wait until I get my powers back. We could live to fight another day."

"While those flies stick a new head on my mom?" Ben asked. "I don't think so!"

If Amber had had the power to cast a spell and make him stay, she would have done so. She knew that fighting was pointless. Her heart was breaking.

"We have more than your mom to worry

about," Amber said. "We have a world of evil to fight. I think that we've lost this battle!"

Suddenly a bird flitted overhead, and at the sound of wings, both of the mice cringed, freezing in place. The bird landed in an orange tree. It was small, harmless. Amber's heart had skipped a couple of beats, but now it slowed back to normal. A second bird shot past, and then a third. A whole flock was coming!

"We haven't lost this battle yet!" Lady Blackpool shouted from above.

Amber whirled. A fearsome-looking red-tailed hawk dropped to the ground behind her, its beak curving down like a reaping hook. Lady Blackpool rode upon its shoulders.

In all of the excitement, Amber had forgotten she was coming!

"Lady Blackpool!" Ben cried, leaping for joy. "Is there room on that thing for three of us?"

"There is," Lady Blackpool said, "so long as you don't thrust me through with that sharp spear of yours."

Ben and Amber pounded through the grass then climbed on the back of the hawk. The raptor leapt into the air.

As it rose and flapped silently between the trees, Ben and Amber told the wizardess of all that they had heard and seen—the trillions of flies ahead, the governor's failed plan to kill them, the vast powers of Belle Z. Bug.

When they got to the part about the giant superflies, Lady Blackpool nodded sagely. "As I have seen in my vision. Always in my dreams, one of them is carrying me to my death."

Lady Blackpool peered forward stoically, as if lost in a nightmare, and then shook her head. "This fly is a great evil. Not since the dimmest times of legend has such a monster been loosed upon the earth. But I am afraid that it pales in comparison to the evils to come."

Amber fell silent. The hawk was flying low over the orange fields. With the setting of the sun, a fresh wind had begun blowing in from the coast, and as night fell and the air cooled, the flies had all begun going to ground.

Not so the birds. Amber checked over her shoulder and watched them leap from the branches of trees and fly ahead in fits and starts. There were tens of thousands of them—flycatchers and bee-eaters, a fearsome army whisking silently through the night.

But she knew that they would not be enough. Belle Z. Bug had her own army of superflies; these birds were no match for such monsters.

All too soon the birds winged out of the orchards and soared over some fields at the edge of the landfill. The garbage rose up in great hills—noxious mounds of old diapers and moldy strawberries, candy bar wrappers and gutted cars. It was as if this were a graveyard, the last remnants of some fallen civilization.

Considering what the flies had done to mankind with their curse of evil, Amber thought, *perhaps it might be the last monument to man.*

The flies had grown quiet now, gone to rest for the night. But Amber conjured visions of burning cities and looted banks, a world where people did evil things just because some nasty little fly whispered for them to do it, with the good folks helpless to disobey.

"Take us down," Lady Blackpool whispered to the hawk, and the great bird soared to the ground and landed without the slightest jolt.

"Get down," Lady Blackpool told Amber and Ben. "This fight is not for you."

Amber knew of Lady Blackpool's destiny. Amber's eyes brimmed with tears. She dropped safely to the ground, and Ben landed beside her.

"Promise me," Lady Blackpool asked Amber, "that when this is done, you will go to S.W.A.R.M."

Amber hesitated. She looked at Ben. She didn't want to go without him. The thought of taking off across the country alone, finding some school in a strange swamp, and meeting odd new magical animals frightened her. But she had fought great evils in the past two weeks, and she found the courage to say, "Yes, I'll go."

Lady Blackpool looked to Ben. "And promise me that when Amber turns you back into a human, you'll have a long and happy life and that you'll always be nice to mice—and all other creatures smaller than you!"

"I'll be nice to mice," Ben said. "But the flies are going to get what they've got coming!"

"Flies are not evil by nature," Lady Blackpool

said. "Icky and disease-ridden, yes, but not evil. Belle Z. Bug has warped their thinking!"

With that, she turned her snout toward the landfill once again, as if she would go do battle. Then she said softly to Amber, "You need to know, Amber, a good wizard only uses magic as a last resort when it comes to resolving disputes. Remember what I said? It is far better to win the hearts of others with reason and gentle persuasion than to use force."

With that she raised a paw in the air and cast a small spell. When next she spoke, her voice came out as a roar, amplified thousands of times over.

Lady Blackpool shouted, "Flies of the world, Belle Z. Bug has sought to seduce your hearts with a lie: she has told you that you are hated by all of the other creatures of the world because flies are ugly. But that is not true.

"The Great Maker, the Master of Field and Fen, created you! Nothing that he has made is ugly or foul. Flies are a masterpiece of intricacy unequaled in all of creation. The Master made you well, and even flies are beautiful.

"The truth is that you are hated because you land on our food and then mop it. You taste our food and then vomit onto it. When you do this, you spread diseases, and you ruin our food. This is why other animals dislike you."

Lady Blackpool's voice boomed and echoed out over the dump, and the flies held still, listening to her attentively. Amber couldn't tell what the flies might be thinking. They weren't like mice. They didn't have any facial expressions. Lady Blackpool continued.

"Stop eating our food!" she pleaded. "Stop being icky, and I'm sure that the rest of the animals will like you better! And for those of you that like to bite: knock it off!

"The truth is that Belle Z. Bug's makeup doesn't truly make you beautiful. It might enhance your natural attractiveness, but you don't need it.

"The truth is that greater beauty can be found within you than upon your surface. Beauty depends more upon what you do than what you look like!"

Lady Blackpool quit her sermon, and her voice boomed out a warning, stern and dangerous. "Flee from Belle Z. Bug!" she roared. "Leave her now, and fly to safety. I give you five minutes, and then the battle begins! All who do not heed my warning: prepare to die!"

Silence fell over the dump. It had not been a stirring speech. It wasn't a rousing masterpiece of oration. Instead Lady Blackpool had made a simple appeal to reason.

Amber hoped that the flies would depart in a great cloud.

Indeed, the dump filled with buzzing as flies rose into the air and nervously began to leave. But not many left—only a thin haze of them.

The remaining flies shouted, "Cowards!" "Turncoats!"

The birds kept winging in, arranging themselves for battle until they covered the ground behind Amber and Ben.

Lady Blackpool shook her head sadly. "The flies have become too invested in evil," she said. "They have bought into Belle Z. Bug's cunning lie, and now they dare not back out."

The birds sat for the full five minutes, sometimes fluttering up in the air for a second to grab a wayward fly. Overhead, darkness had fallen completely, and now stars were beginning to come out. Amber looked up at one lone star, shining bright and indomitable against the encircling darkness.

"The time has come," Lady Blackpool said. She turned to her army of birds. "Take to the skies, my feathered warriors! Eat your fill! Death to the evil flies!"

A roaring wind suddenly burst over the land, shaking the grass and making it hiss. It came from behind, and Amber realized that Lady Blackpool had summoned it with a spell.

The birds lifted off in a rush of wings, speeding toward the dump, the tailwind propelling them swiftly. Lady Blackpool's hawk outraced them all, winging ahead.

A vast cloud of flies rose up to meet them, blotting out the evening stars, blocking the sorceress shrew's path. But her fierce wind cut through the ranks of the flies that could not fight the headwind.

Amber and Ben could hardly tell what happened next. The storm roared in Amber's ears, and the humongous cloud blotted out the stars, bringing on an intense night.

A fierce battle ensued. A bolt of purple lightning rained down out of clear skies, and lances of green lightning seemed to rise up from the earth to do battle with it.

The army of birds swept into the clouds of flies, darting this way and that, shrieking with angry cries and gobbling flies by the tens of thousands.

Eerie lights strobed over the dump. Thunder boomed and rumbled, making the ground tremble as it roared. A column of fire-lit smoke rose up.

"Gosh!" Ben Ravenspell said.

Amber could think of no reply. She'd never been near a battle where two wizards of immense power dueled. She suddenly felt small and insignificant and stupid.

For two weeks she'd been squandering her magical energy, wasting it on frivolous things. But Lady Blackpool had been hoarding her mage dust for decades, growing stronger and stronger, preparing herself to face true evil.

Now the battle was joined, and even from this great distance it was a miracle to behold!

Amber found herself breathless from excitement.

But suddenly the great wind died, and the birds began to chirp in despair. Seconds later, Amber spotted birds whipping overhead in full retreat.

"I think . . ." Ben said, fighting back a sniffle. "I think Lady Blackpool has lost. She's dead!"

Tears welled up in Amber's eyes. She fell to the ground and wept in despair, her heart breaking. More birds whistled overhead, flying away.

"Don't move," Ben whispered. "Maybe our enemies won't see us . . ."

Ben and Amber huddled side by side as birds winged past, followed by clouds of flies.

Suddenly a larger shadow arced overhead then wheeled toward them in a flurry. "Flee!" Lady Blackpool shouted from the back of her hawk. "The battle is lost!"

"You're alive!" Amber cried, jumping up in joy. Ben and Amber hopped to the great hawk and scurried onto its back.

Weary from battle, barely able to cling to the hawk, Lady Blackpool gasped. "Amber," she said. "I've cast my last spell. The wizard wearies are on me, and I can battle no more! Help me hold on, so I don't faint."

So Amber clung to the shrew, and the hawk leapt into the air. It flew swift and sure toward the orange groves then dove beneath the protective canopy of leaves. Fast as a bolt it thundered between the dark boles of orange trees. The smell of fruit was strong and cloying in the darkness.

The hawk veered, and by the time it left the orange groves and went winging toward the stars, the landfill was miles away.

Amber glanced down. She couldn't even see the dump anymore or the cloud of flies. Yet the hawk continued to climb, leaving the danger farther and farther behind.

With every wing-beat, the hawk bore them closer and closer to safety.

Ben began to weep openly. It wasn't some impersonal battle that he had lost. Yes, human civilization was on the brink of ruin, but Ben had lost his own mother.

Amber had come to realize that she liked Mona Ravenspell; silently Amber mourned too.

But the moment was short-lived, for just as they rose up so high that Amber felt that she could reach out from the hawk's shoulder and catch a passing star, she heard a terrible buzzing behind her.

She glanced back just in time to see a trio of giant flies racing up behind.

The hawk let out a frightened screech and tried to dive too late.

A giant fly snagged Amber in its paws and then somersaulted in midair. The monster had her in its clutches!

A moment later, she heard Ben screech, and then two more flies came up behind her. Each fly was carrying one mouse-sized package. Lady Blackpool struggled valiantly to bite her captor, but the monster was holding her by the tail, and she was too weak from battle to reach him.

"Our master seeks your company," Amber's giant fly grumbled. "Don't try to get away. I wouldn't want to drop you!"

"Aaaah," Lady Blackpool moaned. "This is . . . this is just as I saw it in my vision!"

CHAPTER 22

BELLE'S VICTORY BALL

The race does not always go to the swiftest or strongest.
Sometimes it goes to him who outlasts all others.
—LADY BLACKPOOL

In the gathering darkness, a superfly grasped Benjamin Ravenspell.

Ben stabbed the monster in the abdomen, and it hissed and pulled the needle free then tossed it away. Ben watched longingly as it tumbled away, the steel catching bits of starlight, until it was lost in the darkness.

The flies were taking Ben and his friends back to the junkyard one last time. Though he wriggled and tried to break free, it was no use. The superfly held him tightly, and it had the kind of strength that he would expect from such a monster.

Yet as they neared the landfill, Ben saw that something had changed. Fire lit Belle Z. Bug's

193

throne. She'd set hundreds of candles in the masts of the yacht so that it was lit like a Christmas tree.

The flies were still airborne. Billions of followers buzzed softly, a deep and throbbing sound, expectant and watchful. They hovered in the air around the ship.

Ben saw his mother and Governor Shortzenbeggar. Both were still alive, and both of them were being held by superflies.

The light surrounded Belle Z. Bug as if she were on a stage. Immediately Ben recognized what was happening. Belle Z. Bug was going to make an example out of all of them.

Ben's captor landed near Belle and roughly thrust Ben to the deck of the ship. An instant later, Amber and Lady Blackpool were delivered also.

Belle Z. Bug strutted across the deck of her yacht. Her eyes glowed with an evil red light.

"Ah," Belle gloated, "it is so good of you all to come. After all, what is a victory party without a little entertainment? And, of course, you are all so entertaining.

"You know what I'm going to do with you, don't you?" Belle Z. Bug asked.

Ben shook his head.

"I'm going to kill you now. Your bodies will be left out to rot for the night. By morning, your stomachs will have begun to bloat and ooze.

"When you are ready, I am going to lay my eggs in you.

"The maggots that hatch in you will be my

own children. The next generation of fly wizards will gain their nourishment from you.

"But before I destroy you, I want to thank you . . ."

"Thank us?" Lady Blackpool asked in surprise.

"Yes," Belle Z. Bug said. "You waged a fine battle and were worthy opponents. You amused me through what would have otherwise been a long and tedious day.

"You made me sharpen my skills, and you forced me to become my best. I only wish that the Ever Shade had been here. I'm sure that he would have been amused by you, too."

Ben's mother raised her hand.

"Yes?" Belle Z. Bug asked.

"Uh, I'm just an innocent bystander. Can I just get my money out of the Learjet and go?"

"No," Belle said. "I happen to like killing innocent bystanders. In fact, I like killing them so much, I think that I'll execute you first."

"No!" Governor Shortzenbeggar shouted. "Take me first!"

Belle Z. Bug glared at him. "Stop your whining and wait your turn!" she shouted. Then she told the superflies, "Bring the woman!"

The flies had taken Ben's mom by the arms, and though she struggled and tried to break free, they dragged her across the deck of the ship. They threw her down in front of the sorceress fly.

Belle Z. Bug strode forward. "Now, we must decide how to kill you," she said thoughtfully. "It should be something clever, fun . . . something you don't see every day. Oh, and it should be painful and slow, too."

The fly studied Ben's mom and stood above her, absently stroking the charm bracelet around her neck. Once again, Ben noticed it, and felt that it was out of place. Belle Z. Bug was beautiful, with her hot pink carapace color and various forms of makeup. The wing wax on her wings made them glisten like rainbows. The fly-liner and fly-shadow brought out the beauty of her eyes.

But that darned ugly necklace was a puzzle.

Suddenly, Ben got it. The necklace was magic!

He didn't know what it might do, but he knew that it was important—so important that he decided he had to get it from her if it was the last thing that he did!

Belle Z. Bug finished pondering how to kill Mona Ravenspell. "I know: garbage! You humans are so good at making garbage, I think I'll have you eat some. In fact, I'm going to stuff you so full of garbage that it kills you!"

"Oh," Ben's mom said, "a little garbage won't hurt me. I've been eating it all of my life. Believe me, if you'd ever tasted my cooking, you'd know!"

So that's why mom never cooks! Ben realized. She didn't like the taste of her own cooking. Come to think of it, Ben didn't like her cooking, either.

"Oh, you've never tasted garbage like this," Belle Z. Bug warned. "Flies, make me a toxic taco!"

At that, the flies above all began to buzz in glee, and tens of thousands of them raced off in every direction. Moments later, a flock of flies came back with the nastiest flour tortilla Ben had ever seen. Mold grew on it in various shades of gray, green, and blue. Maggots dripped from it as it fell to the deck of the ground with a plop.

Next came the beef: bits of putrid hamburger that had never been cooked, all reeking and rancid. It was so slimy that Ben thought that it might crawl away by itself.

Then came the cheese: limburger. It looked like a perfectly fine piece of limburger, but if you've ever tasted the stuff, you know that it can't be fine.

Then came the condiments—salsa from a grungy old jar, a huge ball of earwax, and various funky-smelling things that Ben couldn't even imagine eating.

The flies gleefully folded the ingredients all together, and they began to chant: "Taco time! Taco time! Taco time!"

The guards that held Ben's mother had her on her knees. Now they forced her head to the ground, and Belle Z. Bug lifted the deadly taco and drew near.

"Get her mouth open!" Belle Z. Bug shouted. "I don't want any of this stuff to spill on me."

The flies began to wrestle with Ben's mom, sticking their fly legs into her mouth, trying to pry it open. She grunted and strained, fighting them as best she could until at last with a growl of despair they got her mouth open.

Ben's mother shouted her dying words. "Ben, I love you! Always remember that I love you!"

Belle Z. Bug growled, "Ah, put a taco in it!" The monster fly shoved the ugly end of the taco toward Mona's mouth.

She screamed and tried to break free. At the last instant, Belle Z. Bug pulled the taco away.

"You really didn't think I was going to give you a good one, did you?" Belle Z. Bug demanded. She bit off the end of the taco, and suddenly Ben realized that to a fly, the toxic taco really would taste good!

Ben looked up to the fly that guarded him. The poor thing was drooling. A great wad of spit plopped on Ben's head.

Belle Z. Bug laughed and waved a hand. Suddenly a new taco magically appeared: one with a fresh handmade tortilla, crisp lettuce, tender slices of corn-fed beef, American cheese, and a zesty pepper salsa.

Belle Z. Bug grasped the taco and shoved it into Mona's mouth. The flies all gasped and recoiled in horror.

Belle Z. Bug had made a terrible miscalculation, and Ben decided to act before she recognized it. The fly that was holding him had loosened his grip just enough so that Ben could slip free.

But he wasn't free to go just anywhere. A billion flies surrounded him. He could never escape.

Maybe I can attack, he thought.

The necklace that Belle Z. Bug wore had caught his eye. Ben wasn't just an ordinary mouse, he was a jumping mouse. More than that, he'd been human once, and he had been studying karate for years.

In a flash, Ben slipped free from his captor. The night air had cooled enough so that the flies moved more slowly, and Ben was able to get two great leaps in before the fly shouted and gave chase.

Two leaps was enough for a Pacific jumping mouse. Ben covered a dozen feet in a heartbeat, veered to his left to avoid the attacking fly, then leapt over his mother and launched himself feet first—right at Belle Z. Bug's throat.

If he'd hit a human there, the kick would have crushed the victim's larynx. It would have made the person's throat swell closed, strangling the victim.

But a fly doesn't have a larynx. A fly breathes through the pores in its carapace and can't be strangled by normal means.

In fact, Ben's kick didn't have much effect at all, except that it broke the charm bracelet Belle Z. Bug wore as a necklace. The elastic string snapped, and charms went scattering everywhere across the deck of the ship.

In that instant, the fly's face grew dull and dusty looking. Her hips grew wide, and a roll of cellulite bulged on her carapace. Her wings drooped like a pair of wilted leaves, and her mop lolled and hung like a sticky piece of taffy.

The flies all around Ben suddenly gasped.

"Ew," one cried. "She's old!"

"Ick," another cried. "She's disgusting!"

"Uh, you guys," a third fly cried, "she's dying."

Sure enough, Belle Z. Bug fell to the ground and began to roll, as flies often will when they're dying.

"My youth," she cried. "My youth! You stole my youth!" The malevolent light that had glowed in her red eyes now began to die. One by one, each of the ten thousand facets in her eyes began to wink out like old light bulbs.

The audience of flies gaped in astonishment.

Lady Blackpool whirled. "Behold your leader!" she said. "Her beauty was a lie, just like her promises! It was not the makeup that made her beautiful but a cunningly wrought spell. All that she had was the beauty of her youth, and now you see her for what she really is!"

"Yuck," the flies cried in horror as she aged. "I'm out of here!" one of the leaders said. "Let's go down to Hollywood and walk around the Boulevard!"

With that, the flies all cheered. Their new leader leapt into the air, and clouds of flies rose up in a swarm and went racing toward Hollywood. Only a couple of the superflies remained, heads hanging dejectedly.

Belle Z. Bug lay on the ground, rolling a bit, then finally landed on her back, her legs waving uselessly in the air. Her eyes had gone blank, with only a couple of dim lights remaining.

Mona Ravenspell and Governor Shortzenbeggar got up and began massaging their wrists. The governor still had an extra fly's head, along with a couple of fly arms and a pair of mismatched wings.

Amber the mouse just stared at the dying fly.

"I . . . don't understand," Amber said. "What happened? Did the governor's poison finally kill her, or was it Lady Blackpool's magic?"

"*Time,*" Lady Blackpool explained. "Time is killing her. Though mice and humans measure life in months and years, Belle Z. Bug was but a fly. A single day is all that she had to live—less than a day. She stored her youth in that necklace and kept it close. So long as it was on her, she could not grow old.

"But now her age has caught up with her, thanks to Ben," Amber said.

Ben stood watching it all, feeling surprised. He had feared that the flies might try to take vengeance on him for killing their master.

He still wasn't entirely sure how he had done it. He decided that he was lucky.

Belle Z. Bug turned her head, and her voice came out as a hiss. "I go now to meet the Master of Field and Fen," she hissed, "and to gain my reward. Nothing can save me. But the Ever Shade is coming, and he shall grant you your reward," she threatened. With smug satisfaction, she added, "and nothing can save *you*!"

Belle Z. Bug's head dropped to the deck of the ship, and she fell silent. Her legs twitched.

It might take hours for her to die, Ben knew. He'd watched one die on the windowsill of his house once. Like a snake, the body of a fly keeps on kicking a little until the heat of the day leaves its body.

So the heroes sat for a bit to watch Belle Z. Bug die. It was a solemn occasion, a lonely vigil, and Ben did not speak. He felt that it was somehow improper or disrespectful.

Finally, one of the superflies, a fine bombardier fly, tilted its head toward Ben's mom. "You will find your treasure inside the shell of the plane, there at the edge of the landfill. You're welcome to it. We flies have no use for it."

"Thank you," Mona said.

The fly turned to Governor Shortzenbeggar. "You, sir, are the finest human on this planet. It was a pleasure defeating you. As your reward, I would like to suggest that you remain a fly. With just a few more alterations, you could become one of us. You would be a handsome specimen, I think . . ."

"That is a generous offer," the governor said, "but I kind of like the idea of keeping the humans' extended life span. No offense, but I don't want to be dead by morning."

The governor's fly head swiveled around. "Hey, speak for yourself, buddy! Have you taken a good look in the mirror? You ain't got nothin' on me! I'm a real ladies' man!"

The governor socked the fly head under the chin. The fly head bobbled back a little as it passed out.

Ben realized that the bombardier fly must be some kind of general or something.

"And now," the bombardier fly said, "you are free to go!"

"Free?" Mona asked. "You're just going to let us go free?"

The bombardier fly shrugged. "Humans make trash, and trash makes flies. There's no value in giving you any extra grief."

Ben wasn't sure that he bought the giant fly's argument. He suspected that it was scared. Two wizards and a vengeful governor are nothing to be toyed with.

Belle Z. Bug's head now rested on the ground. The glowing red lights in her eyes had now nearly all extinguished, and her legs were curled up and folded in on themselves.

Ben's mom came and picked up the mice and put them in her pocket. Then she and Governor Shortzenbeggar climbed down from the garbage mound, hand in hand, walking carefully over a carpet of dead flies lit by the candles that still burned all over the ship like funeral fires. They made their way to the airplane.

Ben sat thoughtfully in his mother's pocket and felt something move near his foot. He peered down and spotted poor, wingless Serena crawling up beside him.

"Is it over?" the butterfly asked.

"Yes," Amber said. "Belle is all but dead."

"Wow, that's a relief," Serena said. "You didn't by chance happen to grab any extra fly-liner for me, did you?"

"No," Ben said.

The group went to the plane, made their way inside, and turned on the emergency lights. As promised, they found all of their money still in the suitcases. The flies had taken all of the bottled water and sandwiches but had left them that.

Ben's mom opened one of the trunks just to be sure, smiled at it kind of sadly, and said, "I wonder if Disneyland will be open tomorrow?"

"I don't want to go anymore," Ben said. "I've had all of the excitement I can handle."

"Me too," Amber said.

"Me three," Serena agreed.

"Me four," the governor chimed in. He took a look at his extra head and said, "and five!"

The group made their way back to the dump truck and drove a few miles until they found Ben's dad and the CIA agents at their field office.

The CIA agents looked up at the governor in confusion. They couldn't seem to decide whether to welcome him back or douse him with fly spray. "Uh, everything under control, sir?" one asked.

"Aye, aye," Governor Shortzenbeggar said.

He shook hands and said good-bye to Ben's mom and dad then shook Ben's paw and Amber's and Lady Blackpool's.

"You'll need some help to get rid of that extra head and appendages," the old shrew told Governor Harold Shortzenbeggar. "I won't be able to cast a spell for a few days, but I'd be happy to help you when I can."

"Oh, thank you for the offer," the governor said. "But I know plastic surgeons in Hollywood that can fix *anything!*"

The governor waved good-bye, and then a CIA agent gave the family a ride to a nice hotel in Malibu.

Ben wasn't sure what to expect at the hotel. Crashed cars littered the freeway, and buildings were smoking from fires. It looked as if all of the state had gone on a riot. But when they got in the lobby, the desk clerk acted as if everything were normal.

"Can we check in?" Butch Ravenspell asked. "I mean, is it all right? Is everything okay?"

"There were some slight . . . irregularities earlier in the day," the clerk said evasively. "But everything seems back to normal."

Ben's dad shoved a wad of money over for the night's stay, and they went to their room. The room was very luxurious, with a hot tub and a big-screen television. The maids had shorted the sheets on the bed and stolen all of the toilet paper and the little chocolates that the guests were supposed to get, but otherwise everything seemed fine.

The whole family ordered dinner at a nice steakhouse down on the main floor of the hotel. Ben's dad got a table right next to a movie star, Jackie Chan, but within minutes, the paparazzi were crawling all over the place, so the whole family was forced to go back to their room early.

Ben's dad called a veterinarian in the phone book, and an animal doctor came right over. Using superglue, she was able to reattach Serena's wings, and within minutes the butterfly was merrily flapping around the room, trying to drink nectar from the flowers in a landscape painting above the bed.

* * *

That night while Ben's mom and dad slept, Amber, Lady Blackpool, and Ben had a little talk.

Amber said to Lady Blackpool, "I thought you were supposed to die tonight. I mean, I'm happy that you didn't, but you seemed so sure . . ."

"I felt sure," Lady Blackpool said. "I was certain that I would die. I have had this vision many times—me being carried to my death. In the vision, I was always certain that I would die. Let this be a lesson to you: dreams and visions might seem certain, but they can never be completely trusted."

Amber seemed relieved. "Does that mean you'll be able to take me to S.W.A.R.M.—now that you're alive?"

"I suppose that since I lived out the day, I'll have to do something," Lady Blackpool agreed. "Yes, I'll lead you to S.W.A.R.M. But first you must turn Ben back into a human and set him free."

"I know," Amber said. She sighed heavily. "Lady Blackpool, I have a question. If I turned myself into a human, could I still go to S.W.A.R.M.?"

Lady Blackpool wiggled her whiskers. "No. It's for small animals only, I'm afraid."

Amber glanced at Ben. He could tell that she wanted him to come with her, and he felt torn. He waited for her to ask once again, to beg, to reason. But her words surprised him: "I'm sorry that you'll have to wait a few more days until I can turn you back into a human. I guess that now, with all that has happened, I've drained my powers even further."

"That's okay," Ben said. "I'm getting kind of used to being a mouse."

It was true—he was getting used to it—but Ben desperately longed to be human again. If nothing else, he wanted to look in the mirror and make sure he wasn't growing facial hair.

But what about life after that? The Ever Shade was coming, and Amber would need to fight him. Ben didn't want to be left out of that adventure, but he wanted to be human, too.

I can always ask my mom and dad for permission to go to S.W.A.R.M., he told himself. But he couldn't imagine them letting him go, and the truth was that he was terrified to go—scared witless—because if he went to S.W.A.R.M., then it would be like enlisting in the army—enlisting to fight the Ever Shade. And if he didn't go with Amber, that might be even worse, because it would be like quitting, like surrendering to the Ever Shade.

Ben was only sure of one thing. He wanted to be human again, if only for a while.

"In three days I'll be human," he told himself hopefully. "Just three more days . . ." But he could not hide from the fact that he knew he had to go to S.W.A.R.M.

EPILOGUE

By the time the Toad Warrior reached the landfill, everything was quiet and dark. Night had fallen, and a few dim stars shone. The candles of Belle Z. Bug's tomb had all but burned out.

Max leapt up close to examine her cold, stiff body.

Overhead, the jets zipped, and in the distance, police sirens could be heard wailing. Max and his companions had found that escaping the police wasn't hard to do. The toads had simply waited until their truck rounded a corner and then leapt out. A small spell kept the truck driving on down the highway, with all of the police cars giving chase.

Max studied Belle Z. Bug for a long moment. "You were a great leader," he said to her cooling body. "The plan goes as it should, and the Ever Shade will be grateful. The flies that you raised shall feed my armies for weeks to come, and when your eggs hatch, your children will be fearsome warriors indeed."

One of Belle Z. Bug's legs twitched, and a single red light glowed like a coal in her faceted eyes.

"Most importantly," the Toad Warrior added, "your power will now be mine!"

With that, he zipped out his tongue and grabbed Belle Z. Bug, swallowing her whole. She was huge, almost as large as him. But Max used his magical powers to suck her in.

Now, he thought, *her magic will join with mine, making me stronger than ever! Let the world tremble and shake.*

With that, the Toad Warrior let out a mighty croak—a croak so loud that it shook the earth.

Everywhere around the world, toads stopped in their hunts or crawled from their hiding places, eyes blinking, and set off immediately to join their evil master.

A NOTE FROM
THE AUTHOR

If you liked this book, do the author a favor and tell a friend!

There may soon be a movie going into production for *Of Mice and Magic*. You can find out the latest news about this and upcoming books from the series on the web at http://www.benravenspell.com/